# Early Life
## Leadership Workbook

101 Strategies to Grow Great Leaders

Christina DeMara

All Rights Reserved
*Early Life Leadership Workbook: 101 Strategies to Grow Great Leaders*
Published by DeMara-Kirby & Associates, LLC
Printed in the United States of America

United State Library of Congress
© 2017 Christina DeMara
All material in *Early Life Leadership Workbook: 101 Strategies to Grow Great Leaders,* including all intellectual ideas, methodology, materials, pictures, and graphics on these pages, are copyrighted by DeMara-Kirby & Associates.

All rights reserved. No part of these pages, either text or image, may be used for any purpose other than personal use. Therefore, reproduction, modification, storage in a retrieval system, or retransmission, in any form or by any means, electronic, mechanical, without written permission from the author is prohibited without prior written permission from DeMara-Kirby & Associates and Christina DeMara. General inquiries should be directed to customer service via

christinademara.com.
Disclaimer: *Early Life Leadership Workbook: 101 Strategies to Grow Great Leaders* is based on the research, professional opinion, and experiences of the author, and it does not promise anything to the reader.

CHRISTINA DEMARA
LIFE · LEARNING · LEADERSHIP

# Early Life Leadership Books & Resources

## Early Life Leadership in Children
101 Strategies to Grow Great Leaders

## Early Life Leadership
101 Conversation Starters and Writing Prompts

## Early Life Leadership Workbook
101 Strategies to Grow Great Leaders

## Early Life Leadership Workbook for Girls
101 Strategies to Grow Great Leaders

## Early Life Leadership Kids Journal

## Early Life Leadership in the Classroom
Resources, Strategies & Tidbits to Grow Great Leaders

# Table of Contents

Early Life Leadership Books & Resources ............................................. iii

A Note to the Reader .............................................................................. xi

7 Things This Book Intends: ................................................................. xii

Acknowledgments .................................................................................. xiii

Early Life Leadership Pledge ................................................................ xiv
Reflect & Complete ................................................................................ xv
   101 Strategies to Grow Great Leaders ........................................... 1
   **1.** Strategy Leaders Are Open-Minded: ........................................... 3
   **2.** Strategy Leaders Include Everyone: ............................................ 4
   **3.** Strategy Leaders Give Feedback: ................................................. 5
   **4.** Strategy Leaders Do Not Give Up: .............................................. 6
   Reflect & Complete ............................................................................. 7
   **5.** Strategy Leaders Communicate Effectively: ............................... 8
   **6.** Strategy Leaders Acknowledge the Ideas of Others: ................ 9
   **7.** Strategy Leaders Manage Money Effectively: .......................... 10
   Reflect & Complete ........................................................................... 11
   **8.** Strategy Leaders Read to Be Better: ........................................... 12
   **9.** Strategy Leaders Run for Election: ............................................ 13
   Reflect & Complete: .......................................................................... 14
   **10.** Strategy Leaders Problem-Solve: ............................................. 15
   **11.** Strategy Leaders Are Always Working
        on Resiliency: ............................................................. 17
Reflect & Complete .............................................................................. 18
   **12.** Strategy Leaders Are Humble: ................................................. 19
   **13.** Strategy Leaders Reflect: ........................................................... 20
   **14.** Strategy Leaders Put Themselves in Other
People's Shoes: ................................................................................... 21
   **15.** Strategy Leaders are Positive: .................................................. 22

**16.** Strategy Leaders Know How to Give Recognition: ............ 23
**17.** Strategy Leaders Brainstorm: ................................................ 24
**18.** Strategy Leaders Are Courageous: ...................................... 25
**19.** Strategy Leaders Collaborate: .............................................. 27
Reflect & Complete ........................................................................ 28
**20.** Strategy Leaders Compare and Contrast: ......................... 29
**21.** Strategy Leaders Encourage Others to
      Do the Right Thing: ......................................................... 31
**22.** Strategy Leaders Value Other Languages: ........................ 33
**23.** Strategy Leaders Care about Their Communities: .......... 34
**24.** Strategy Leaders Are Empathic: .......................................... 35
**25.** Strategy Leaders Think, and Think, and Think Again: ...... 36
**26.** Strategy Leaders Formulate Ideas: ..................................... 37
**27.** Strategy Leaders Encourage Team Activities: .................. 38
**28.** Strategy Leaders Do Not Believe in Entitlement: ............. 39
**29.** Strategy Leaders Set Goals: ................................................. 40
**30.** Strategy Leaders Learn from History: ................................ 41
Reflect & Complete ........................................................................ 42
**31.** Strategy Leaders Motivate: .................................................. 43
**32.** Strategy Leaders Don't Leave Anyone Out: ..................... 44
**33.** Strategy Leaders Listen: ....................................................... 45
**34.** Strategy Great Leaders Have Great Mentors: ................. 46
**35.** Strategy Leaders Know There Is Always More
      Than One Way to Get Things Done: ............................ 48
**36.** Strategy Leaders Understand the Importance
      of Creativity: ..................................................................... 50
**37.** Strategy Leaders Know There Is a Time and
      Place for Everything: ....................................................... 51
Reflect & Complete ........................................................................ 52
**38.** Strategy Leaders Read for Leisure: .................................... 53
**39.** Strategy Leaders Forgive: .................................................... 55
Reflect & Complete ........................................................................ 56
**40.** Strategy Leaders Learn from the Past: .............................. 57
Reflect & Complete ........................................................................ 58
**41.** Strategy Leaders Respect Knowledge: .............................. 59

Reflect & Complete ................................................................ 61
**42.** Strategy Leaders Love What They Do: ............................... 62
**43.** Strategy Leaders Know How to Share Power: ................... 63
**44.** Strategy Leaders Are Selfless: ........................................... 65
**45.** Strategy Leaders Hold Themselves Accountable: ............. 67
**46.** Strategy Leaders Are Proactive: ........................................ 68
**47.** Strategy Leaders Believe in Spirituality: ........................... 69
Reflect & Complete ................................................................ 70
**48.** Strategy Leaders Are Slow to Anger: ................................ 71
**49.** Strategy Leaders Know the Small Things Count: ............. 72
**50.** Strategy Leaders Understand Social Equality: .................. 74
**51.** Strategy Leaders Keep It Real: ......................................... 76
**52.** Strategy Leaders Have Collections: .................................. 78
**53.** Strategy Leaders Take Charge: ........................................ 79
**54.** Strategy Leaders Set Personal Growth Goals: .................. 80
**55.** Strategy Leaders Look at Things from Different
       Perspectives: ..................................................................81
**56.** Strategy Leaders Have Hobbies: ...................................... 82
**57.** Strategy Leaders Are Globally Aware: .............................. 83
**58.** Strategy Leaders Govern Effectively: ............................... 84
**59.** Strategy Leaders Help: ..................................................... 87
**60.** Strategy Leaders Collaborate in Decision Making: ........... 89
**61.** Strategy Leaders Encourage Change: .............................. 90
**62.** Strategy Leaders Are Self-Aware: .................................... 92
Reflect & Complete ................................................................ 93
**63.** Strategy Leaders Present: ................................................ 94
**64.** Strategy Leaders Know the Importance
       of Current Events: ......................................................... 95
**65.** Strategy Leaders Reward Optimistic Thinking: ................ 96
Reflect & Complete: ............................................................... 97
**66.** Strategy Leaders Self-Reflect: .......................................... 99
Reflect & Complete ................................................................ 100
**67.** Strategy Leaders Have Honest Thoughts: ....................... 101
**68.** Strategy Leaders See the Good in ALL People: ............... 103
Reflect & Complete ................................................................ 104

**69.** Strategy Leaders Know How to Enjoy Their
   Time Off: ................................................................105
The icons are examples ..............................................106
**70.** Strategy Leaders Have Good Manners: ....................108
**71.** Strategy Leaders Understand the Importance
   of Honor: ..............................................................109
**72.** Strategy Leaders Understand There Are Always
   Consequences to Their Actions: ............................110
**73.** Strategy Leaders Understand the Difference between
   Management and Leadership: ...............................112
**74.** Strategy Leaders Understand the Importance
   of Denying Gratification: .....................................114
Reflect & Complete ...................................................115
**75.** Strategy Leaders Understand the Art of Persuasion: ....124
**76.** Strategy Leaders Seek Advice: ..................................125
**77.** Strategy Leaders Lead by Example: ..........................127
**78.** Strategy Leaders Are Teachable: ...............................129
**79.** Strategy Leaders Embrace Opportunity: ...................130
Reflect & Complete ...................................................131
**80.** Strategy Leaders Understand the Importance
   of Being Healthy: ..................................................140
**81.** Strategy Leaders Give Compliments: ........................141
Reflect & Complete ...................................................142
**82.** Strategy Leaders Persevere: .......................................143
**83.** Strategy Leaders Know the Importance of Building
   Negotiation Skills: ................................................144
Reflect & Complete ...................................................145
**84.** Strategy Leaders Reward Their Team Members: .......146
**85.** Strategy Leaders Do Not Participate in Favoritism: ....147
**86.** Strategy Leaders Can Say No Respectfully: ...............148
**87.** Strategy Leaders Roll Up Their Sleeves and
   Get to Work: .........................................................149
Reflect & Complete ...................................................150
**88.** Strategy Leaders Are Diligent: ..................................151
**89.** Strategy Leaders Practice Confident Communication: ....152

**90.** Strategy Leaders Understand Loyalty: ...................................153
**91.** Strategy Leaders Love Life: ....................................................154
**92.** Strategy Leaders Follow the Rules: ........................................155
**93.** Strategy Leaders Give the Whole Team Credit: ..................156
**94.** Strategy Leaders Understand the Power of Words: ..........157
**95.** Strategy Leaders Wear All Kinds of Different Hats: .......158
**96.** Strategy Leaders Are Compassionate: ...................................159
Future Leadership Goals Checklist............................................160
**97.** Strategy Leaders Understand the Importance of
 a Good Tribe: ............................................................161
**98.** Strategy Leaders Know They Cannot Control
 Others, Only Themselves: ........................................162
**99.** Strategy Leaders Love What They Do: ..............................163
**100.** Strategy Leaders Respect Differences: ................................165
**101.** Strategy Leaders Reflect: ........................................................166
Bonus!..............................................................................................167

Free Copy of the.................................................................................167

DeMara Reflection Grid ....................................................................167

Bibliography .......................................................................................171

About the Author................................................................................181

# A Note to the Reader

Dear Valued Reader,

I am writing this letter to congratulate you on taking the first step into the future. Leadership is all around us. As you go through this workbook, you will learn and see how leadership affects your everyday life. I gave birth to this workbook after a lot of intense research on children, youth, personality, and leadership. I believe everyone has the potential to make a positive impact in the world. I felt the need to give back to the world something I believe in so strongly. I wrote this book with you in mind. You are the future of a better world. Being a leader isn't easy. Some activities in this book might be easy for you and some might be difficult. Nevertheless, never give up on being the best you! If we want a better tomorrow, we must rise up, make a change, and do what is right! I hope you continue to grow in leadership. I hope you continue to read. I hope you continue to explore who you are. But most importantly, I hope you continue being you! God bless you.
With gratitude and warm wishes,

CHRISTINA DEMARA
LIFE · LEARNING · LEADERSHIP

# 7 Things This Book Intends

1. To help teach and help others understand leadership skills.
2. To build leaders through higher-level thinking, questioning, and activities, as a group or independently.
3. To teach self-monitoring by using the graphics to create a mental picture and leadership understanding.
   For example, on or near the up arrow, students will write what they need to increase in order to be a better leader. On or near the down arrow, students will write what needs to be stopped or limited in order to reach their leadership potential.
4. To increase awareness of leadership in hopes of potentially gaining more leadership opportunities that will carry over to college and career.
5. To be used as a reflection tool.
   Later, Early Life Leaders can go back and see how they have grown and what they have learned.
6. To be used as a supplemental tool for academic camps, Bible studies, STEM programs, and extracurricular activities.
7. To build mentorships and professional relationships with trusted adults, coaches, teachers, and mentors as they complete this Early Life Leadership book together.

# Acknowledgments

To each reader: dream, believe, achieve!

This book is dedicated to my beloved family,
and to all the underdogs.

Underdogs, rise and make a difference!

Thank you, God, for your grace!

# Early Life Leadership Pledge

**READ & BELIEVE!**

"I am a strong, ethical leader!
I do what is right even when it's not easy!
Every day, I want to grow and learn! I can make a difference!"

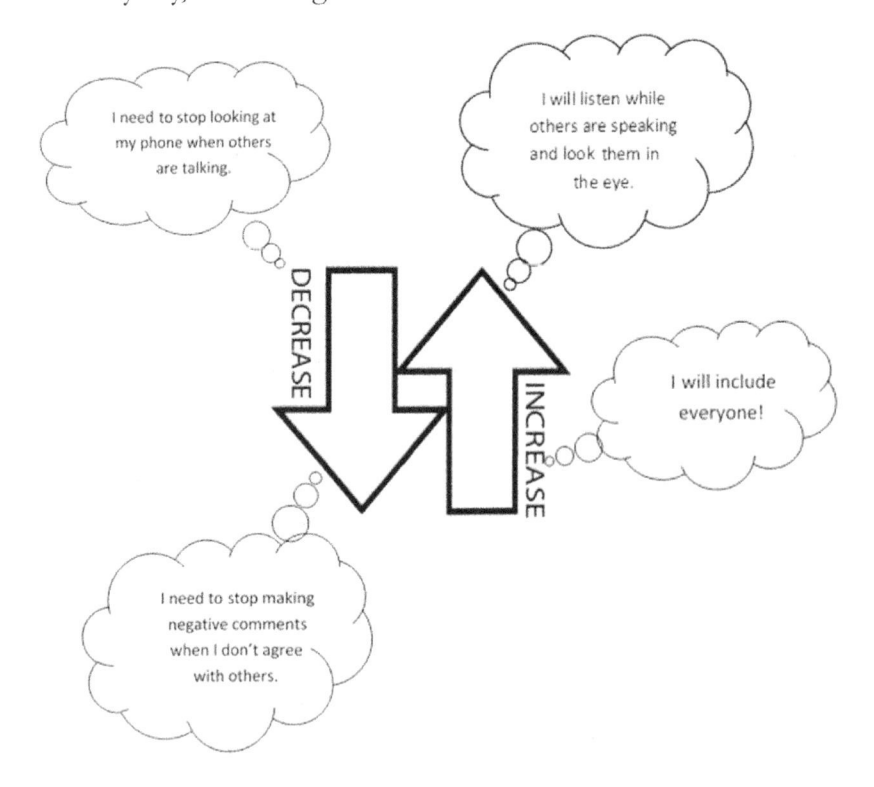

- I need to stop looking at my phone when others are talking.
- I will listen while others are speaking and look them in the eye.
- I will include everyone!
- I need to stop making negative comments when I don't agree with others.

**DECREASE** ↓ / **INCREASE** ↑

# Reflect & Complete

Take a few minutes to reflect.

Later in the book, you will come back to this.

| K | E | W | L |
|---|---|---|---|
| What do I **know** about leadership? | What is my leadership **experience**? | What do **I want** to know about leadership? | What have I **learned**? |
|  |  |  |  |

# 101 Strategies to Grow Great Leaders

# 1. Leaders Are Open-Minded

When we are open-minded, it allows others to express their thoughts and ideas without criticism.

**WHY IS THIS IMPORTANT?**

If we criticize others, they will be less likely to share their thoughts because they will want to dodge feelings of rejection and the fear of being wrong. We must listen, be respectful, and try to see things from other perspectives.

**RECOMMENDATION:**

Praise others when their ideas are good, and guide others when their ideas are bad or unachievable. For example: You could say, "That's a great idea, but we only have this to work with. Can we come up with more ideas?" This keeps everyone involved in the thinking process.

## What do you need to increase or decrease to be more open-minded?

# 2. Leaders Include Everyone

*R*ecognize and include everyone in activities despite individual giftedness, disability, or unique social backgrounds.

**WHY IS THIS IMPORTANT?**

No one likes to be left out. It hurts, even for adults. You can learn a lot through social interaction, so make sure you are including and learning from everyone.

**RECOMMENDATION:**

There are many opportunities during the school day to include everyone. Be a leader and make sure you include other students warmly during group activities.

## What can you increase or decrease to include everyone in activities?

# 3. Leaders Give Feedback

When we give each other feedback, we recognize others' accomplishments. Effective praise and constructive criticism help others recognize the good they have done, and it guides them toward what needs to be changed.

**WHY IS THIS IMPORTANT?**

By giving feedback, we are learning how to value the information of others. When we give feedback, we are saying, "I hear you and have given thought to your valuable information." That is a powerful thing!

**RECOMMENDATION:**

There are a few ways you can learn to give feedback: (1) give feedback layers, state something positive, then the negative, and end with a positive, (2) give someone feedback and include two solutions, and (3) share different examples of feedback you have received, maybe a note from a boss, teacher, customer, friend, or family member and talk about how it made you feel.

## Have you ever received feedback on your behavior or academics?

## How did it make you feel?

_____
_____
_____
_____
_____
_____
_____

# 4. Leaders Do Not Give Up

When we keep trying to accomplish a goal and move forward with determination, this makes us good leaders.

**WHY IS THIS IMPORTANT?**

Leaders always give it all they got. Leaders never give up. Not giving up doesn't always mean that we are successful, but as we move forward, we are forced to reflect, think strategically, and solve problems.

**RECOMMENDATION:**

Talk about times when you did not give up on something and share your triumphs and failures.

### What keeps you going when you want to give up?

### What do you need to increase or decrease in order to not give up when times get hard?

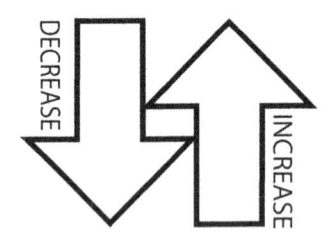

*Early Life Leadership Workbook*

# Reflect & Complete

Talk about a time you helped a friend who was frustrated and wanted to give up. When we get upset or do not like an activity or sport, it's crucial to understand that it's okay to be angry or disappointed. When you are calm, talk about what went right and what went wrong. Come up with a new game plan and remember that giving up is not an option going forward. Leaders don't give up.

**Use the lines below to take notes.**

# 5. Leaders Communicate Effectively

When leaders communicate effectively, they can vocalize a clear message and correct errors without put-downs.

**WHY IS THIS IMPORTANT?**

As leaders, we are not going to get anyone to follow us if we cannot communicate effectively.

**RECOMMENDATION:**

There is several components to communicating effectively: (1) paint a clear picture— "What do I want?" and "What am I trying to say?"; (2) balance positive and constructive feedback— "What do I need to change?" and "What should I keep doing?"; and (3) be positive, always recognizing strength in the situation or person— "What are some good things going on?"

## What are some things I need to increase or decrease to communicate effectively?

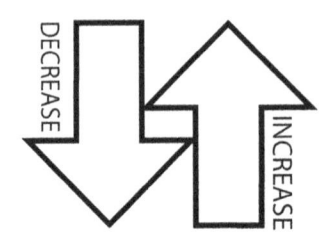

# 6. Leaders Acknowledge the Ideas of Others

**A**cknowledging the ideas of others displays your appreciation for your teammates' ideas.

**WHY IS THIS IMPORTANT?**

As leaders, we do not know everything, nor should we take credit for someone else's ideas or hard work. Acknowledging the ideas of others shows we are humble, open-minded, and committed to being part of a team.

**RECOMMENDATION:**

It is okay to not know everything and it's okay to not always have the best ideas

### How do you show others you acknowledge their ideas?

_____
_____
_____
_____
_____
_____

# 7. Leaders Manage Money Effectively

Managing money effectively means that all financial responsibilities are being met, with minimal debt, and there is a cushion for an emergency.

**WHY IS THIS IMPORTANT?**

Understanding money management allows you to learn to budget and to learn from small financial mistakes now rather than later as adults. As you grow up to be a leader, you will be managing retirement money, college funds, and money from your jobs. It is important you learn to manage money correctly.

## What are behaviors you can increase or decrease to help manage money effectively?

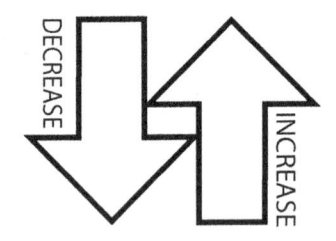

# Reflect & Complete

**MANAGING MONEY EFFECTIVELY:**

My favorite learning experience for students is fundraising. Fundraising provides a valuable math lesson. Make a list of some things you want. Prioritize the items on your list from the most important to the least important. Think about and articulate what is more important and come up with a plan for how to save for it and earn money for it. This will help you understand what you can and can't afford.

1. _____
   _____
   _____

2. _____
   _____
   _____

3. _____
   _____
   _____

4. _____
   _____
   _____

5. _____
   _____
   _____

# 8. Leaders Read to Be Better

If you study successful leaders, they will all tell you they read. You do not have to read storybooks all the time. Try reading something you are interested in like recipe books, sports stories, biographies, and how-to books.

**WHY IS THIS IMPORTANT?**

Reading meaningful literature will help you form your ideas about the world, different cultures, and most importantly what leadership is and looks like. This will set the foundation for lifelong learning and life experiences.

**RECOMMENDATION:**

Use books to learn about life and leadership. Exposing yourself to a variety of literature will help demonstrate leadership and model leadership-like behavior. Leaders are well rounded and know a little something about everything. You can read books with family and friends and ask open-ended questions. For example, "Why did he do that? How do you know he was a good leader? Which character in the book is the leader and why?"

## What are some genres you like and why?

_____
_____
_____
_____
_____
_____

# 9. Leaders Run for Election

Elections encourage youth-based politics and help develop students into great leaders.

**WHY IS THIS IMPORTANT?**

A good old-fashioned school campaign can teach you a lot of leadership lessons. The biggest takeaway from a school election should be that youth can learn the importance of becoming advocates for their peers.

**RECOMMENDATION:**

Many schools and groups have organizational committees and leadership positions. For example, Boy Scouts and Girl Scouts of America have leadership roles, public schools have class officers, and athletic teams have captains.

## How can you step into a leadership position?

## What do you need to increase and decrease in order to encourage youth-based politics in your life?

# Reflect & Complete

### STRENGTHS AND WEAKNESSES

On the left side of the circle note your strengths. On the right, note your weaknesses, and the overlapping part in the middle are potentialities. Potentialities are skills that are noted as not quite mastered yet but have the potential to be strengths.

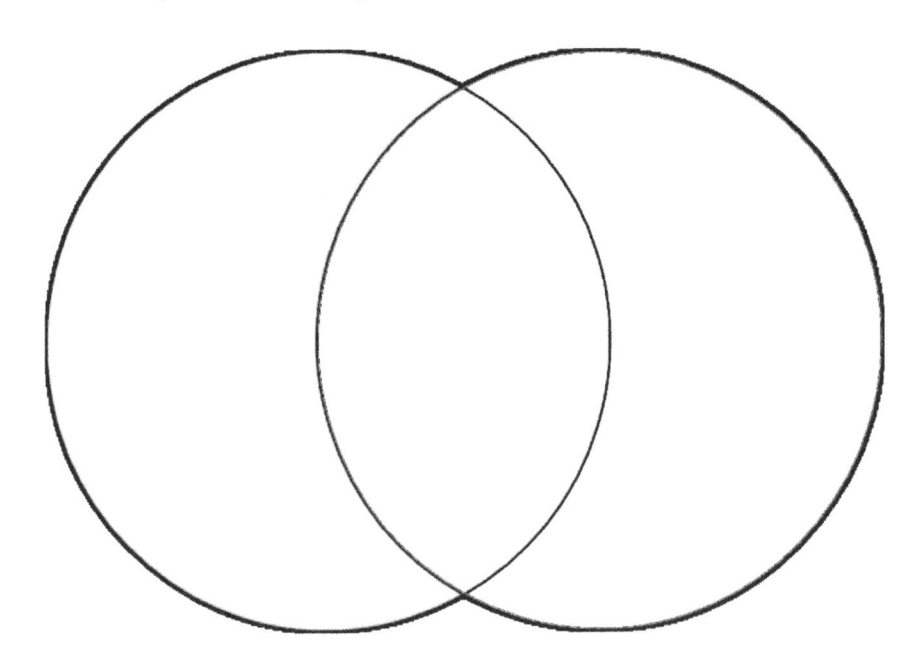

# 10. Leaders Problem-Solve

Leaders understand the importance of identifying a problem and then brainstorming the different solutions and how they affect others.

**WHY IS THIS IMPORTANT?**

Everyone sees dilemmas and solutions differently. This is a learned behavior. Seeing dilemmas and solutions differently will help condition you to troubleshoot and problem-solve independently throughout life.

**RECOMMENDATION:**

We often keep our thinking to ourselves. Instead, try troubleshooting and problem-solving aloud. Include your family, friends, or teammates. First, explain to them the problem, and then give some possible solutions to help fix the issue. Guide your thinking through open-ended questioning. For example: "Why do you think that's a good idea? How else can we fix this?"

### Reflect on a time you had a problem you had to troubleshoot.

### How did you solve it? What worked and what didn't?

I found that… _____

_____
_____
_____

Early Life Leadership Workbook

🧠 I solved my problem by... _____
_____
_____
_____

🧠 This worked... _____
_____
_____
_____

🧠 This didn't work... _____
_____
_____
_____

# 11. Leaders Are Always Working on Resiliency

Resiliency is the capacity to get over difficulties quickly and to spring back into action. When we take professional or personal hits, it always hurts, even for adults. Sometimes, we instantly jump back up, and sometimes, we are injured, and it takes time to heal our wounds.

**WHY IS THIS IMPORTANT?**

Resiliency is something that always varies, according to the situation. The brutal hits from life never stop coming, no matter how old we get. It is crucial that we pride ourselves on "getting back up" no matter how small or big the hit. It could be a lost friendship, a bad game, or a bad grade. No matter what it is, we all find it hard to be resilient at times.

**RECOMMENDATION:**

Reflect on a time in your life when you had to be resilient.

## How do you get over difficulties quickly and spring back into action?

_____
_____
_____
_____
_____
_____
_____

# Reflect & Complete

**Who are the people in your life who are resilient and why?**

_____
_____
_____
_____
_____

**What was one of the hardest things you have had to face? How did you get back up?**

_____
_____
_____
_____
_____

**What can you do or tell someone to help them get back up when they are feeling defeated?**

_____
_____
_____
_____
_____

# 12. Leaders Are Humble

*B*eing humble is essential for one to lead effectively. I always use the car analogy. For example, all the parts on a car are necessary to get the car running efficiently. Great leaders humbly know that everyone is important, from the janitor to the president of the company.

**WHY IS THIS IMPORTANT?**

Humbling yourself will create mutual respect among the people around you.

**RECOMMENDATION:**

Lead by example, apologize when you should, and remember it's okay to admit you don't know everything.

## How can you be humbler?

## What do you need to increase or decrease?

## When have you been humble or experienced a humble leader?

# 13. Leaders Reflect

It's important to think about the different things going on in our lives. When we reflect, we are intentionally thinking about something specific, such as a good or bad experience. When we reflect, we are considering either what went on during the experience or our feelings to learn from that specific experience.

**WHY IS THIS IMPORTANT?**

Reflection encourages high levels of thinking, enables learning from the good and bad, and helps us be better leaders.

**RECOMMENDATION:**

Guide reflection discussions with friends or family, asking open-ended questions. For example: "Why do think that happened? What do you think we should change? How do you know it was bad?" Other recommendations include leadership journals or drawing pictures.

## How can you increase the reflection process in your life?

## What are some leadership experiences you can reflect on?

# 14. Leaders Put Themselves in Other People's Shoes

Putting ourselves in other people's shoes helps us understand why people behave in a variety of ways.

**WHY IS THIS IMPORTANT?**

We can't expect to understand why people do what they do, but we can teach them to understand that all people are different and react differently.

**RECOMMENDATION:**

When we put ourselves in other people's shoes, we are trying to feel what they are feeling, and we are trying to see things the way they see them. Words do wonders! Saying to someone that we understand goes a long way! "I am trying to put myself in your shoes" also says, "I respect you and how you think and feel."

- Listen to what the person is saying.
- Think about what I heard.
- Think about how the speaker feels.
- Think about why they have specific feelings.
- Be respectful when I respond.

# 15. Leaders are Positive

When things do go right, how do you respond? Great leaders say, "I can," not "I can't."

**WHY IS THIS IMPORTANT?**

As leaders, we set the example. Nothing ever goes as planned. Leaders don't say negative comments like, "We are never going to reach our goals." They say the opposite: "Okay, what do we need to change to meet our goals?" Leaders make other positive comments like, "Great job! We can do this! Keep the positive energy going!"

**RECOMMENDATION:**

Take the three-day challenge! Do not say anything negative for three days. This means you cannot criticize, put anyone down, or be critical of others.

**Do you know people who always complain and say negative comments?**

**How does it make you feel? What do you need to change in your life to be more positive?**

# 16. Leaders Know How to Give Recognition

Recognizing the people around you creates value and respect for their work.

**WHY IS THIS IMPORTANT?**

By acknowledging others, we are creating a positive environment. This is a useful leadership tool that creates an environment where people are compelled to give their best.

**RECOMMENDATION:**

Some examples of recognition can be a handwritten note or an announcement. Create cards or draw pictures. This will help reinforce the relationship between words and letters along with making others feel good.

How does it feel to give recognition?

_____
_____
_____
_____

How does it feel to receive recognition?

_____
_____
_____
_____

# 17. Leaders Brainstorm

*B*rainstorming is a process that helps us achieve a goal or fix a problem.

**WHY IS THIS IMPORTANT?**

Brainstorming is extremely important because we do this daily. Technology is changing lightning fast. We need to be able to brainstorm, and problem solve an array of problems to keep up with everything going on around us.

**RECOMMENDATION:**

Changing the end of a story is a great way to practice brainstorming. For example: The tortoise won the race, so what could the rabbit have done to win? What if there were five bears and only three bowls of porridge? This will serve as a great brainstorming exercise that can be done in the car on the way home from school.

## How can brainstorming help you, and how can you increase brainstorming in your daily life?

# 18. Leaders Are Courageous

Courageous people can take a stand and advocate for themselves or for the people they care about.

**WHY IS THIS IMPORTANT?**

As leaders, sometimes we stand alone in decision-making, advocating, or defending something we believe in. It takes courage to stand up for something you believe in. It takes courage to report bullying. It takes courage to leave a situation when people are doing bad things.

**RECOMMENDATION:**

Some courageous examples could include political or spiritual people in history or in the community. For example: Mother Teresa, Cesar Chavez, Dwight D. Eisenhower, or Rosa Parks. Many books give great examples of courage.

What does courage look like?

_____
_____
_____
_____
_____
_____
_____

🧠 Who are some people in your life who demonstrate courage?

_____
_____
_____
_____
_____
_____
_____

🧠 What makes you courageous?

_____
_____
_____
_____
_____
_____
_____

# 19. Leaders Collaborate

*B*y working in groups, we are giving everyone the opportunity to contribute to the process.

**WHY IS THIS IMPORTANT?**

In the real world, we go to school with others, work with others, and interact with others daily. Although interaction occurs, that does not mean it's always pleasant; there is a difference between interaction and collaboration. Collaboration is proactive because it is intended to be enjoyable, welcoming, and provide a learning experience.

**RECOMMENDATION:**

When collaborating with others: (1) be positive and give the opportunity to work with others a chance, (2) be respectful by listening, and (3) be open-minded about new ideas and learning new things.

## What can you learn by collaborating with others?

## How can you increase collaboration when you are in a group, and no one knows each other?

*Early Life Leadership Workbook*

# Reflect & Complete

### THE LEADERSHIP LADDER:

I developed this graphic organizer to help students brainstorm different ways to meet their goals. Write three strategies to complete your goals. In the small area, note your emotion behind each goal. For example, confident, unsure, or excited.

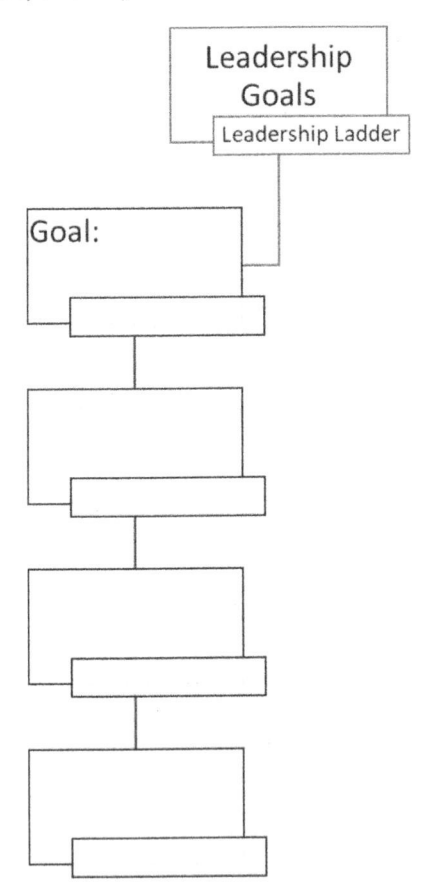

```
          ┌─────────────┐
          │ Leadership  │
          │   Goals     │
          ├─────────────┤
          │Leadership Ladder│
          └─────────────┘
  ┌──────────────┐
  │ Goal:        │
  │              │
  └──────────────┘
       ┌──────────────┐
       │              │
       └──────────────┘
  ┌──────────────┐
  │              │
  │              │
  └──────────────┘
       ┌──────────────┐
       │              │
       └──────────────┘
  ┌──────────────┐
  │              │
  │              │
  └──────────────┘
       ┌──────────────┐
       │              │
       └──────────────┘
  ┌──────────────┐
  │              │
  └──────────────┘
       ┌──────────────┐
       │              │
       └──────────────┘
```

# 20. Leaders Compare and Contrast

Great leaders can differentiate between the positive and negative and between similarities and differences in situations.

**WHY IS THIS IMPORTANT?**

Learning how to compare and contrast in everyday situations is crucial because it causes us to think and learn.

**RECOMMENDATION:**

This can be done through discussion, analyzing the behaviors of story characters, and asking open-ended questions that force us to analyze our *own* behaviors, which is the highest level of thinking. We may not get there overnight, but that is the goal.

## Can you compare and contrast your leadership capabilities?

What are some of your leadership strengths?

_____
_____
_____
_____
_____

What are some of your leadership weaknesses?

_____
_____
_____
_____
_____

# 21. Leaders Encourage Others to Do the Right Thing

Leaders understand that sometimes doing the right thing is hard, and they inspire others to do what is right.

**WHY IS THIS IMPORTANT?**

Throughout life, we will constantly be at a crossroad with good and bad. It is not only important that we know right from wrong, but as leaders, it is essential that we encourage others to do the right thing.

**RECOMMENDATION:**

This can be done through modeling. My son was upset with me because I was "making" him take advanced classes in high school. He wanted to take the regular classes with some of his friends, so he did not have to set forth any effort. He wanted to take the easy road. It wasn't the right thing to do. He was smart and more than capable. I had to explain to him that he needed to take the advanced classes because it was the right thing to do, and maybe he could encourage some of his friends to challenge themselves.

Have you ever encouraged anyone to take a better road?

_____
_____
_____
_____
_____
_____

What do you do to keep yourself motivated to do the right thing?

# 22. Leaders Value Other Languages

Two languages are better than one!

**WHY IS THIS IMPORTANT?**

We live in a global world full of different people and languages. Knowing two languages can help you be more desirable when looking for a job in a demanding global market. Knowing more than one language is a great thing for a global market, and it can preserve heritage and create an appreciation for other cultures.

**RECOMMENDATION:**

Some might say, "I'm not bilingual, so how can I learn to speak another language?" Learning another language can be taught at home via YouTube, through bilingual programs at your local school, or at a learning center. There are also language programs online. Something to think about and research is American Sign Language. It is a great second language that promotes diversity.

Do you know two languages? Who are some people in your family or in your circle of friends that can help you learn a different language?

_____
_____
_____
_____
_____

# 23. Leaders Care about Their Communities

We should all understand that caring is going above and beyond when there is no obligation to do so. Caring for your community should be a regular part of your life.

**WHY IS THIS IMPORTANT?**

Caring about the community helps us understand that sometimes there are problems bigger than ourselves, and there are needs out there bigger than our own.

**RECOMMENDATION:**

Get involved in activities such as donating to or volunteering at hospitals, churches, daycare centers, nursing homes, soup kitchens, or nonprofit organizations. Donating does not always mean money; it can be your time or toys and clothing you have outgrown. Finding a need in the community and helping to fulfill it brings so much gratification to life. We definitely need to feel this!

## How can you increase your community involvement?
## How can you encourage others?

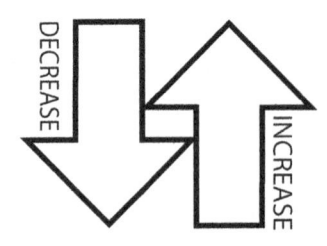

# 24. Leaders Are Empathic

**E**mpathic leaders can share another person's feelings.

**WHY IS THIS IMPORTANT?**

Empathy doesn't mean weakness. Empathy is important because it helps us put ourselves in someone else's circumstances, and through that, we can lead more effectively and build stronger relationships.

**RECOMMENDATION:**

Encourage emotional sensitivity through discussion. When you do not agree with someone or understand their thinking, try to put yourself in their shoes. "How do you think Jake feels? Why did you think he feels that way?" It only takes a few minutes to build this skill.

## What are some situations where you might have to be empathetic?

## What do you need to increase or decrease to be more empathetic towards others?

# 25. Leaders Think, and Think, and Think Again

Thinking is a more complex process than we realize. Companies spend tons of money on teaching staff how to problem solve and troubleshoot.

**WHY IS THIS IMPORTANT?**

As humans, we are never perfect. Thinking is part of growing. For us to grow as leaders, we need to reflect on the good, the bad, and the ugly. When we stop thinking, we stop growing.

**RECOMMENDATION:**

Think about leadership, and draw a picture of what leadership looks like without using words. Pass them around to teammates and think about what you are seeing. Share your thoughts and ideas with your team. After you share, you can write a story that connects leadership to the pictures.

## What can you do to increase your creation of ideas, brainstorming, and thinking?

# 26. Leaders Formulate Ideas

Young people are idea generators when given the fertile soil to flourish. We can acquire a lot of knowledge from each other. We need to listen to everyone's ideas. When we shut people down, it can be hurtful and stunt their creativity. Instead, guide them; encourage brainstorming and the sharing of ideas.

**WHY IS THIS IMPORTANT?**

Some of our biggest inventions can benefit from a small idea. Think of the light bulb, television, iPhone, and electric cars. Leaders are always looking to make things better with their ideas.

**RECOMMENDATION:**

Keep a journal or an online word document of ideas. It is always great to go back and reflect and add.

**Think about great leaders and the things they have created or invented, like computers and airplanes.**

**Who are some leaders with great ideas that have changed the world?**

_____
_____
_____
_____
_____

# 27. Leaders Encourage Team Activities

Leaders understand being part of a team is essential.

**WHY IS THIS IMPORTANT?**

As we grow up and join the workplace, we are consistently working with people. Working with others as a team is essential if we are going to lead effectively.

**RECOMMENDATION:**

Think about joining group activities. You may want to consider joining a scout troop or participating in sports teams, school band, book clubs, dance, cheer teams, and hobby-based clubs. We can all learn valuable lessons about teamwork through these activities.

### What are team activities you have experienced?

### What was difficult and what was easy?

### What did you learn?

_____
_____
_____
_____
_____

# 28. Leaders Do Not Believe in Entitlement

Merriam-Webster describes entitlement as a feeling or belief that you deserve to be given something (such as special privileges). Entitlement is toxic, especially when working in a team or group.

**WHY IS THIS IMPORTANT?**

The importance of this stems from the belief that we are all important and have something to contribute. Leaders understand how important their team is to their business. Feeling entitled is not going to get leaders anywhere.

**RECOMMENDATION:**

Do not say "I" in a group; encourage saying "we." This a very hard thing for some people to learn or identify. Use your words wisely, for example; you could high-five someone in your family and say, "We make a great team. Now we all need to clean up." You can practice this. No one should be immune to hard work or pitching in.

## Why is it hard to work with someone who feels entitled?

## What can you learn from that situation?

_____
_____
_____
_____
_____

# 29. Leaders Set Goals

Setting goals will help you be successful in life.

**WHY IS THIS IMPORTANT?**

Setting a goal teaches a lot of different things, such as dedication, hard work, perseverance, focus, and time management.

**RECOMMENDATION:**

Make sure goals are attainable, and dates are set for completion. Journaling is great to keep track of a goal journey; pictures can be drawn of goals and ideas and timelines.

## What are some things you can do to increase your chances of meeting your goals in your life?

## What do you need to decrease in your life to accomplish your goals?

# 30. Leaders Learn from History

*H*istory is a great place to explore leadership.

**WHY IS THIS IMPORTANT?**

Exploring historical leaders is important because not only do we need to understand their contributions, or learn from their mistakes, but most importantly, we need to understand their leadership journeys in the context of their lives.

**RECOMMENDATION:**

There are many age-appropriate books. Explore leaders in your areas of interest. Think through the different experiences, contributions, and biographies of great inventors, athletes, musicians, female leaders, artistic leaders, and political leaders. Not all historical leaders were politicians. Discuss some leaders who made a difference in history. My favorite leader in history was Amelia Earhart. She was an American aviation specialist and author!

## Who are some great leaders from your past or history?

## Why were they great leaders?

_____
_____
_____
_____
_____
_____
_____

## Reflect & Complete

Cause and effect is a great way to analyze why things happen. The cause will be the action taken by the adult. The effect will be the action displayed by the child. For example, the adult let the child guide family game night. The effect was the child threw a tantrum when the child felt things were not going his way. This exercise will help you pinpoint what was and wasn't the cause, so we can go back and look at the different stages of Early Life Leadership.

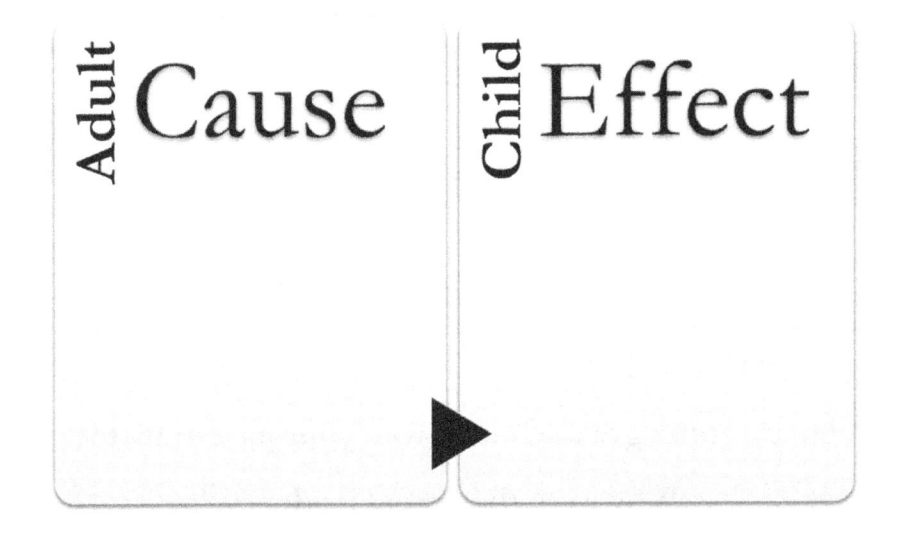

**Adult: Cause** ▶ **Child: Effect**

# 31. Leaders Motivate

When we are motivated, we are more productive and satisfied. It is essential that leaders keep their followers motivated and motivate themselves.

**WHY IS THIS IMPORTANT?**

Motivation is important because it makes followers feel good, and it gives them the gas to keep going and accomplish their goals.

**RECOMMENDATION:**

State testing in public schools is a realistic accountability measure. I think it is great when students make posters and cards for students who are testing. This is an excellent way to teach and encourage motivation. Learning how to give sincere praise and motivate the people around you is important. For example: You could say to a family member, "You did a good job with dinner. You should cook more often." or "I liked your answer!" Give two people a supportive comment.

## How can you increase your self-motivation?

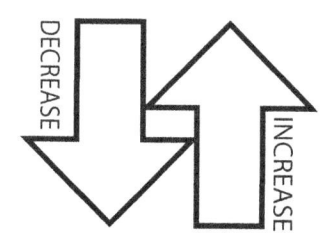

# 32. Leaders Don't Leave Anyone Out

Just like with a car, great leaders understand that ALL components are essential for the car to move and get going in the right direction. It hurts to be left out, even for adults. When parts of the car are missing, we can't get very far.

**WHY IS THIS IMPORTANT?**

When everyone is included, it sends several messages: (1) we are a team, (2) everyone matters, and (3) we all have something to offer. This creates diversity, respect, and leadership.

**RECOMMENDATION:**

Invite everyone to be part of your team or group. Always encourage the opportunity to include everyone and talk about how it feels to be left out.

## Have you ever been left out?

## How did that make you feel?

_____

_____

_____

_____

_____

# 33. Leaders Listen

When we listen, we show unsaid respect for the speaker.

**WHY IS THIS IMPORTANT?**

In the work world, listening is important because leaders cannot be everywhere at the same time, so leaders rely on followers for information. Listening not only shows respect, but it leads to fewer misunderstandings, it enables more learning, and it gives the leader time to reflect on what the other person is saying.

**RECOMMENDATION:**

Youth can demonstrate leadership and listening skills by participating in activities such as team sports or dance groups. It is important to develop listening skills through our activities.

## What does listening look like?

## How do you feel when you know someone is listening to you?

## How does it make others feel when you are listening?

_____
_____
_____
_____

# 34. Great Leaders Have Great Mentors

Leaders learn from the people around them. A mentor is a good, trustworthy friend with a lot of experience who coaches us through life or through our professional career. Many times, we will find someone who has already been in the direction we are headed. Mentors can include family members, coaches, community volunteers, and people in your church.

**WHY IS THIS IMPORTANT?**

A great mentor is priceless, especially if that person is skilled in an area you have an interest in as well. A mentor can guide, motivate, and inspire greatness in us. On the other hand, it is also important to mentor others too. We receive help, and we give help.

**RECOMMENDATION:**

Learning from others is a great thing. Also, giving your help without being asked is just as great. Sometimes older students are paired with younger students to tutor or to help with a sport or activity. Both the mentor and mentee enjoy the experience and are learning.

Why would you be a good mentor?

_____

_____

_____

_____

_____

## What do you have to offer?

_____
_____
_____
_____
_____
_____

## What did you learn from your mentors?

_____
_____
_____
_____
_____
_____

# 35. Leaders Know There Is Always More Than One Way to Get Things Done

Everyone is different and does things differently. We must embrace that, learn from one another, and be open to different ideas.

**WHY IS THIS IMPORTANT?**

Understanding there is more than one way to accomplish something is important because when we collaborate with others in a group or on a team, people might do things differently. And that's okay. Remember, every experience is a learning experience.

**RECOMMENDATION:**

Doing things differently on purpose and out of routine is a great start. For example: We do not have a dinner routine. We eat something different every night. Everyone in the family has an opportunity to pick recipes and cook.

What are some things you do differently than other people?

_____
_____
_____
_____
_____
_____

What are some things you would like to mix up and do differently?

_____
_____
_____
_____
_____
_____

How do you come up with different ideas?

_____
_____
_____
_____
_____
_____

# 36. Leaders Understand the Importance of Creativity

Great leaders are creative and think outside the box. Go out of your way to create, design, make, and complete different types of projects.

**WHY IS THIS IMPORTANT?**

Promoting creativity is a great way to increase thinking, problem-solving, and creative opportunities.

**RECOMMENDATION:**

Projects can range from writing poems, making thank-you cards, writing short stories, developing skits, videotaping events, painting, building with Legos, journaling, cooking, baking, and doing supervised woodwork. Creative projects are also a good way to relax and rejuvenate.

**What are some things you like to do to increase your creativity?**

# 37. Leaders Know There Is a Time and Place for Everything

Sometimes, it is okay to be funny, and sometimes we need to sit respectfully, listen, and focus on what is in front of us.

**WHY IS THIS IMPORTANT?**

Knowing there is a time and a place for everything is essential for leading. It is impossible to stay in an ivory tower and expect followers to respect and trust your leadership. Leaders never put anyone down or brutally correct followers in front of others.

**RECOMMENDATION:**

Role-playing is an excellent way to adjust, practice and polish our behavior. Think about how we should act in different situations.

### Has there been a special event, interview, banquet, or situation that you have had to prepare for?

### What did you do to prepare?

_____

_____

_____

_____

# Reflect & Complete

David has three rambunctious boys who love their trampoline, soccer, and wrestling shows. David has been preparing the boys for his sister's upscale wedding in Colorado for over a year. He role-plays with the boys. He models, "This is how we sit at the table. If someone offers you something and it looks gross, you simply say, no thank you." He reminds the boys that making throw-up noises is not acceptable at a wedding, but they can make them in the backyard. Everyone learns differently and will learn at different paces, but we must all be taught first.

# 38. Leaders Read for Leisure

Great leaders read just for fun.

**WHY IS THIS IMPORTANT?**

Most successful people will say they enjoy reading. I have heard many, such as Mark Zuckerberg, Bill Gates, and Oprah Winfrey, say they read at least one book a month.

**RECOMMENDATION:**

Teaming up with others to trade books or create a reading club is a great way to encourage reading.

What are some books that have inspired you or that you enjoyed?

_____
_____
_____
_____
_____
_____

What are your reading interests about the world, recipes, and adventures?

_____
_____
_____
_____
_____
_____

How can technology help increase your reading?

# 39. Leaders Forgive

Often, we associate forgiving with weakness. That could not be further from the truth.

**WHY IS THIS IMPORTANT?**

Throughout our lives, people will let us down. Forgiving isn't always for the other person. Forgiving helps us heal. It is very hard to lead and be successful if we are angry and resentful.

**RECOMMENDATION:**

In a group or with a partner, demonstrate forgiveness by modeling. For example:

JOHN: Sara, I am sorry I cut a piece of your hair. Will you please forgive me?
SARA: Yes, John, I can forgive you. Thank you.

**It isn't always this smooth. Forgiving others shows your character, strength, and professionalism.**

**What does forgiveness look like, and why is it important?**

_____
_____
_____
_____
_____

*Early Life Leadership Workbook*

# Reflect & Complete

This list was simply designed to reflect. Add your notes on the lines below. You can return to them over time.

### Leadership Skill:

_____
_____
_____

### How do I use this skill?

_____
_____
_____

### How is this skill working in my life?

_____
_____
_____

### Where do I use this leadership skill in my life?

_____
_____
_____

### How can I improve this leadership skill?

_____
_____
_____

# 40. Leaders Learn from the Past

There are two ways leaders learn from the past: (1) by the mistakes of others and (2) by their own past mistakes.

**WHY IS THIS IMPORTANT?**

Learning from something that went wrong in our lives is important. It prevents us and others from making the same mistakes.

**RECOMMENDATION:**

It is important to learn and understand the effects of your actions on your future endeavors by: (1) studying past historical and famous leaders, (2) Reflect & Complete, or (3) talking and drawing pictures of mistakes and articulating why they were wrong.

# Reflect & Complete

What are some experiences from your past that you have learned from?

___

# 41. Leaders Respect Knowledge

It is our personal responsibility to take off the horse blinders. We need to put down our phones and expose ourselves to diverse knowledge and experiences in different areas, such as people, food, countries, cultures, traditions, games, arts, and music.

**WHY IS THIS IMPORTANT?**

As leaders, we need to be a generation that is respectful and knowledgeable of differences in the world. That can only be done if we respect and seek different types of knowledge.

**RECOMMENDATION:**

I experienced this with friends who have different traditions, or religious beliefs. I also have friends who have different preferences for books and academic favorites. Some of my friends love math, and some don't. When we respect knowledge, we listen with an open mind, make eye contact. We never call people names or make negative comments.

Why is respecting knowledge important?

_____
_____
_____
_____
_____
_____
_____

What are some different types of thinking, information, ideas, and knowledge that you have respected?

___

What does respecting knowledge look like?

# Reflect & Complete

With technology, there are so many ways we can now obtain knowledge. There are many websites like the History Channel, PBS, and National Geographic. Other methods for acquiring different types of knowledge include phone applications, Google searches, museums, culturally diverse restaurants, exploring other countries, literature, and recipes. Some book clubs explore components of culture, art, and music, which you could present to your classmates and family. Where do you get knowledge from, and what does that knowledge look like?

_____
_____
_____
_____
_____
_____
_____
_____
_____
_____
_____
_____

# 42. Leaders Love What They Do

*L*eaders understand they can only lead successfully if they are passionate about what they do.

**WHY IS THIS IMPORTANT?**

Passion is something we grow to learn and understand. Passion gives meaning and direction to our lives and careers.

**RECOMMENDATION:**

Teaching passion to students is a little difficult because passion is an abstract concept. Look around at the people in your life, in books, or in movies and shows. Think about the lives of athletes and scientists.

## How can you increase love and value for the things in your life?

# 43. Leaders Know How to Share Power

As leaders, we don't always lead alone. We often share our leadership role with others or in the form of a committee or team. When you give others the chance to lead, you are building future leadership, empowerment, and trust.

**WHY IS THIS IMPORTANT?**

Sharing power is important because it creates ownership and shared responsibility. As leaders, we are not always the most knowledgeable about an area, and we don't always have all the answers. It is important to surround yourself with a diverse team and encourage them to contribute and lead.

**RECOMMENDATION:**

In a group or with a partner, think about the leaders in your life. How have they empowered you to be a great leader? Maybe it was a family member, teacher, pastor, coach, or boss who gave you the opportunity to lead.

What are some experiences you have had with sharing leadership with others?

_____
_____
_____
_____
_____
_____
_____

Who was the first person who encouraged you to be a leader?

# 44. Leaders Are Selfless

Great leaders will put the needs of their followers first.

**WHY IS THIS IMPORTANT?**

Everyone wants to feel valued and protected. We tend to follow someone who is selfless and gives us a sense of protection, appreciates our hard work, and makes us feel secure. When we have a selfless leader who respects us, our job satisfaction and productivity increase.

**RECOMMENDATION:**

Think about characteristics or people you have known who have admirable qualities that make them selfless. For example: Consider parents who sacrificed for family, disabled individuals who led productive lives, and AmeriCorps volunteers who leave comfort and security to help others.

How can you make yourself a better selfless leader?

_____
_____
_____
_____
_____
_____

## Early Life Leadership Workbook

What do you need to increase and decrease?

___

What does selflessness look like?

___

# 45. Leaders Hold Themselves Accountable

Great leaders with a strong sense of self-awareness accept responsibility for the things that go well and the things that go wrong in their lives.

#### Why is this important?

Accepting responsibility for your actions is a very mature thing. This is something that you will need to do throughout your life in a work setting and in your everyday relationships.

#### Recommendation:

Accountability can be taught through intentional discussions, team sports, literature, and modeling.

## What does accepting responsibility for your actions look like?

DECREASE ⬇  INCREASE ⬆

# 46. Leaders Are Proactive

Reactive behavior is when we react due to an action or event. Proactive behavior is when we plan beforehand to prevent anything from going wrong.

**WHY IS THIS IMPORTANT?**

Being a proactive leader means we have thought out our plans thoroughly and have a Plan A and a Plan B. Being proactive is an awesome thing because you are learning to think ahead and problem-solve.

**RECOMMENDATION:**

Take time to plan ahead. When things don't go right, put a positive light on things. Develop a Plan A and a Plan B for one goal in your life.

**When have you been proactive in your life, and what were the benefits?**

**What are the repercussions for not planning ahead?**

_____
_____
_____
_____
_____
_____
_____

# 47. Leaders Believe in Spirituality

We all should know and feel the unsaid law of the universe, which I call Right and Wrong. Great leaders believe in something and find strength in it.

**WHY IS THIS IMPORTANT?**

Spirituality is important because we all need to believe in something, or else why are we here? Why are we trying to make a difference? Why are we trying to be better leaders? Leaders find peace, renewal, and direction in their spirituality, and they believe that spirituality will ultimately make them better.

**RECOMMENDATION:**

No matter what or whom you believe in, understanding the goodness in the world through positive behaviors, cultures, and environments reminds us how to treat people well and with respect. Even a handshake, saying please and thank-you, and a big smile go a long way in letting your spirituality and goodness shine through!

## How does your spiritually affect your leadership?

_____
_____
_____
_____
_____
_____

# Reflect & Complete

What are the things in your life that are helping you grow? Make notes or draw inside the tree.

# 48. Leaders Are Slow to Anger

Anger is a strong emotion that creates strong feelings and sometimes regrettable actions.

**WHY IS THIS IMPORTANT?**

Being slow to anger is very important for leaders. Many times, the things that anger us are misunderstanding or beyond our control.

**RECOMMENDATION:**

Prepare yourself! With a partner or in a group, role-play a misunderstanding or a situation where someone else might be angry. For example: "I am upset because someone took my snack without permission." "I hear what you are saying. Let's try to fix this." Or here's another example: "You aren't being fair!" "Okay, let's talk it out."

**Think about a time you were angry. How could you have handled it better?**

**How can controlling your temper help you as a leader?**

_____
_____
_____
_____
_____
_____
_____
_____

# 49. Leaders Know the Small Things Count

Great leaders acknowledge the small things that lead to growth and movement in the right direction. Little things like doing things before you are asked to, being polite, and giving every day 100 percent goes a long way.

**WHY IS THIS IMPORTANT?**

When applying to a college or for a job, what is going to separate you from everyone else? It is important to go the extra mile in everything you do.

**RECOMMENDATION:**

(1) Ask your family, mentors, and tribe questions. For example, "What do you think?" and "How can I do this better?" (2) Do everything to the best of your ability. (3) Stay positive and be polite.

What are little things you do to make situations better?

_____
_____
_____
_____
_____
_____

What are some small things you can do as a leader to make others feel appreciated?

_____
_____
_____
_____
_____
_____
_____
_____
_____

# 50. Leaders Understand Social Equality

When we understand social equality, we treat everyone with respect, from the janitor to the CEO.

**WHY IS THIS IMPORTANT?**

Treating everyone with the same respect is imperative when you are leading. This can help establish trust and respect.

**RECOMMENDATION:**

With a partner or group, role-play what treating each other with respect looks like.

How can social equality be useful in your life now and later in adulthood?

_____
_____
_____
_____
_____
_____
_____
_____

What does social equality look like?

# 51. Leaders Keep It Real

Leaders who keep it real are genuine and transparent in who they are to those around them.

**WHY IS THIS IMPORTANT?**

When we like our boss or teachers, we tend to try harder. We don't mind going the extra mile. When we "keep it real," we are transparent about who we are. Others are getting to know us, and that builds trust and respect.

**RECOMMENDATION:**

Due to peer pressure, "keeping it real" can be a tricky thing. We have all been shown right and wrong. There are tons of media coming at us, telling us who we are and what we should look like. Always be true to who you are. No one is perfect. Remember, we all have things we wish we could change.

How does "keeping it real" help you accomplish your goals?

_____
_____
_____
_____
_____
_____
_____

What does transparency look like?

# 52. Leaders Have Collections

All leaders collect something. It may be books, shoes, cars, or antiques.

**WHY IS THIS IMPORTANT?**

Collections are important because they help create responsibility and ownership.

**RECOMMENDATION:**

Turn your interests into a collection, share a current collection, or interview a relative or family friend about theirs. Some inexpensive collections can be snow globes, postcards, keychains, pens/markers, T-shirts, etc.

**What are some things you have collected, and why are they valuable to you?**

_____
_____
_____
_____

# 53. Leaders Take Charge

*F*ind a need in your community or local organization that needs to be fulfilled and take charge of it!

**WHY IS THIS IMPORTANT?**

Although leaders can't change the world overnight, we can take charge and fulfill one need at a time. Take charge and focus on one thing at a time. It is better to take charge and execute one thing than to have a lot of unfinished projects.

**RECOMMENDATION:**

On campus or at home, take charge of something small, such as picking up trash every week for beautification, collecting socks and shoes for the less fortunate, or starting a recycling club at school. This is a great way to take charge. Any small deed makes the world better!

## What is something you would like to take charge of in your school, community, or church?

## What does taking charge look like?

_____
_____
_____
_____
_____
_____

# 54. Leaders Set Personal Growth Goals

Talking about and reflecting on one's future is a great thing!

**WHY IS THIS IMPORTANT?**

Great leaders never stop growing and learning. It is essential to start this habit at an early age.

**RECOMMENDATION:**

A good way to work on personal growth is by researching the types of people you admire. For example: Research information about a pilot, college professor, doctor, computer engineer, or veterinarian. Who are the best people in this area and why? By studying the best, we can help ourselves grow.

## What careers are you considering, and how are you going to get there?

## What can you do to be a better leader in your field of interest?

_____
_____
_____
_____
_____

# 55. Leaders Look at Things from Different Perspectives

Leaders understand the importance of seeing things from everyone's perspective.

**WHY IS THIS IMPORTANT?**

As humans, we instinctively do what we think is best for us. It just might be part of our innate programming to survive, but in today's world, as leaders, we need to put ourselves in other people's shoes, especially our followers, and look at things from different perspectives.

**RECOMMENDATION:**

Think about a problem, and then think about how different people would solve it. For example: Your school wins ten thousand dollars; how should the school spend it? Think about this scenario from different perspectives, such as that of the school principal, students, parents, local business owners, and teachers.

## Why is looking at things from different perspectives difficult?

## What do you need to increase or decrease to have a better perspective on things?

# 56. Leaders Have Hobbies

Leaders have hobbies because it's a good way to turn off work and redirect your energy.

**WHY IS THIS IMPORTANT?**

Hobbies are fulfilling and relaxing, and it's during those hobbies that sometimes leaders come up with the best ideas!

**RECOMMENDATION:**

Some families have hobbies like running and biking. Other individual hobbies are great too, such as painting, baking, restoring cars, and gardening.

## What are some of your hobbies?

## How do your hobbies help you be a stronger leader?

# 57. Leaders Are Globally Aware

Great leaders understand and respect that there are different people, cultures, and languages all over the world.

**WHY IS THIS IMPORTANT?**

Global awareness is important because we live, work, and study within a melting pot of races and backgrounds.

**RECOMMENDATION:**

Because the United States is a melting pot, we have access to different food, museums, clothing, events, libraries, and most importantly, people.

**With a partner or group, share three interesting things or traditions about your culture.**

**What can you increase in your life to be a more global leader?**

# 58. Leaders Govern Effectively

The Merriam-Webster Dictionary defines govern as "to watch over someone, and the interest of their or others' security."

**WHY IS THIS IMPORTANT?**

None of us want to be governed by a leader who does not have our well-being or best interest in mind. As leaders, we oversee things at work and home. By starting this at an early age, we are increasing our chances of governing ethically and effectively in adulthood.

**RECOMMENDATION:**

There are three ways you can learn to govern: (1) in your classroom, group, or team, establish a code of rules for behavior, (2) volunteer to take charge of something or a task in your classroom or home, and (3) try teaching or coaching little kids.

## What are some things that current leaders need to increase to lead effectively?

Set a leadership goal in the middle. Add things that will help you reach your goal. See the example below. Create your own on the next page.

**HIT YOUR TARGET!**

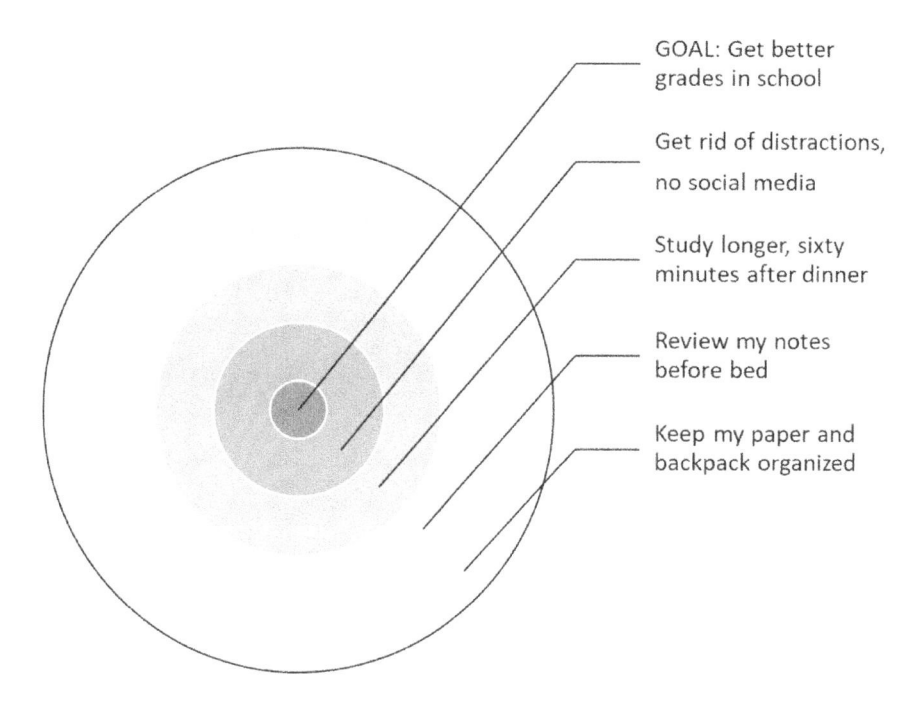

GOAL: Get better grades in school

Get rid of distractions, no social media

Study longer, sixty minutes after dinner

Review my notes before bed

Keep my paper and backpack organized

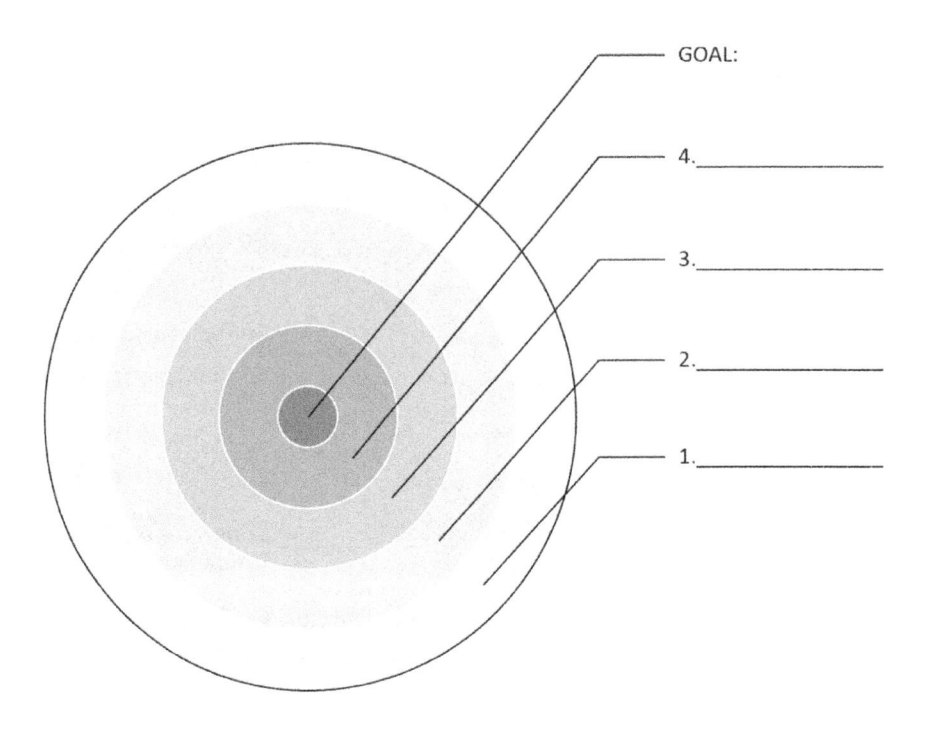

Early Life Leadership Workbook

GOAL: _____

4. _____

3. _____

2. _____

1. _____

# 59. Leaders Help

We all need to learn at an early age that helping feels better than being served.

**WHY IS THIS IMPORTANT?**

As leaders, we should be the first to help and the last to be served. As leaders, we need to make sure everyone around us has what they need to be successful.

**RECOMMENDATION:**

Model what help looks like to others. Be intentional with your words. Give positive reinforcement: "Thank you for helping me with these bags. You are a great helper." "I saw how you helped that lady with the door. That was nice of you." Take advantage of opportunities to help and serve your family and community.

What does helping look like?

_____
_____
_____
_____
_____
_____
_____

## Early Life Leadership Workbook

🧠 What are some things that are important to you to help with?

_____
_____
_____
_____
_____
_____
_____

🧠 How does helping others make you feel?

_____
_____
_____
_____
_____
_____
_____

# 60. Leaders Collaborate in Decision-Making

Decision-making is a hard thing to do alone. Getting advice from a trusted adult or committee input can help.

**WHY IS THIS IMPORTANT?**

Collaborating in decision-making is a great thing. It is important when making a decision to get a committee. When decisions are based on consensus, you are sharing the responsibility, creating buy-in, and including some people whom the decision affects. The collaboration will also help with execution because it is agreed upon by more than just one person.

**RECOMMENDATION:**

In your classroom, in your community, or with your team, you can gather data to help make decisions. Surveys, bar charts, and graphs are a great way to look at information.

## What was one of the most difficult decisions you have had to make?

## Why was it difficult, and who helped you?

_____
_____
_____
_____

# 61. Leaders Encourage Change

Leaders are not too intimidated to push the first domino of change.

**WHY IS THIS IMPORTANT?**

Everything changes and great leaders aren't afraid to try new things with their businesses. Think about the iPhone. Apple is always trying to make a better phone. Employers are looking for leaders who can accept change and help others transition through change.

**RECOMMENDATION:**

An excellent way to learn how to encourage change is to study solutions to real-life problems. With a partner or group, think about a problem you have and what you need to change to fix it.

What is one of the biggest changes you have faced, and why was it difficult?

_____
_____
_____
_____
_____
_____
_____

Why is change hard for some people?

# 62. Leaders Are Self-Aware

Do you know who you are? Self-awareness means you have an honest understanding of your strengths, weaknesses, life principles, and belief system.

**WHY IS THIS IMPORTANT?**

Without an honest understanding of who you are as a leader, you will never be trusted or respected by others.

**RECOMMENDATION:**

Reflect on what leadership skills and abilities you need to have mastered and why. I recommend using sentence stems, such as, "I am a good leader because...," and "I need to improve . . . to be a better leader."

# Reflect & Complete

Call three people and ask them, "What are one of my strengths and one of my weaknesses?"

| I called: | 📞 | 📞 | 📞 |
|---|---|---|---|
| My strength: | ✓ | ✓ | ✓ |
| My weakness: | ✗ | ✗ | ✗ |

# 63. Leaders Present

Take opportunities to present or speak in front of others.

**WHY IS THIS IMPORTANT?**

Speaking in front of others is essential because it prepares us for bigger and better opportunities as we get older and more experienced. Colleges and companies are looking for well-spoken students and employees. Some will have problems with presenting; for others, this will be easy. Practicing early will help us reach our potential and sharpen our presenting skills.

**RECOMMENDATION:**

Participate in a public event where you speak, present, or perform. Presenting in front of classmates is also a great start!

## Why is presenting in front of others so hard, and what helps you stay calm when you're presenting in front of others?

_____
_____
_____
_____
_____
_____

# 64. Leaders Know the Importance of Current Events

Leaders understand the importance of knowing what is going on in the community and in the rest of the world.

**WHY IS THIS IMPORTANT?**

There is so much going on in the world. These events and historical moments in time affect everything around us and impact our decisions making.

**RECOMMENDATION:**

Read the newspapers or news feeds online. Talk about what you read with a friend or trusted adult. Think about all the different perceptions without judgment.

## What can you do to increase your awareness of current events?

# 65. Leaders Reward Optimistic Thinking

Leaders know that optimism is linked to success.

**WHY IS THIS IMPORTANT?**

Optimism creates positive energy; people are drawn to optimistic people. It is important to encourage optimism in the people around you.

**RECOMMENDATION:**

Try to go a day, three days, or a week without saying anything negative. You can only respond using positive comments.

## What are some things that can increase your optimism?

## What do you need to decrease to be more optimistic?

# Reflect & Complete

### WHAT DO LEADERS POST ON SOCIAL MEDIA?

Stay away from posting inappropriate language and pictures. Colleges and employers will check your accounts. Leaders post important events, accomplishments, and anything positive. Social media should always represent you at your best. What do your posts look like?

### FACEBOOK

_____
_____
_____
_____
_____
_____
_____
_____

### SNAPCHAT

_____
_____
_____
_____
_____
_____
_____
_____

## Instagram

## Twitter

# 66. Leaders Self-Reflect

Leaders think about who they are to make themselves better.

**WHY IS THIS IMPORTANT?**

Self-reflection is important because it allows you to accept responsibility when things go wrong. Without self-reflection, we cannot grow, learn new things, and self-correct.

**RECOMMENDATION:**

You can: (1) think about what leadership traits you have and whom you have inherited them from, (2) talk to your friends and family to identify your strengths, and (3) reflect on different situations you have been in.

What are some ways you are thinking about reflecting?

_____
_____
_____
_____

Did you know that talking to a trusted friend or family member can be a great way to reflect? Who can you talk to and why?

_____
_____
_____
_____

Early Life Leadership Workbook

# Reflect & Complete

Below, fill in the leadership skill you would like to infuse. Secondly, note different strategies and things you can do to learn and sharpen your leadership capabilities.

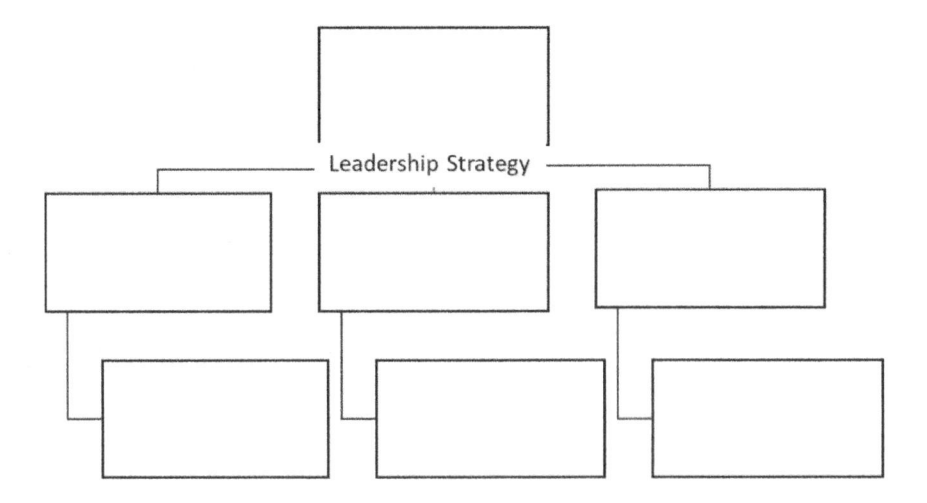

**LEADERSHIP SKILL**

Leadership Strategy

# 67. Leaders Have Honest Thoughts

*H*onest thoughts guide us to do the right things.

**WHY IS THIS IMPORTANT?**

Having honest thoughts is important because honesty always wins. When you have honest thoughts, you do the right things. When you believe that people have honest intentions, you establish trust and create a positive environment.

**RECOMMENDATION:**

Honest thoughts can be a very difficult process for youth, but remember we were born honest and pure. This skill is something that takes time. Talk to your family and friends about a time they were honest about something. In a group: (1) define honesty, (2) describe with verbs what honesty looks like, and (3) talk to three trusted adults about how they have been honest in their lives.

When we have honest thoughts, we give everyone the benefit of the doubt. What does that mean and look like?

_____
_____
_____
_____
_____
_____
_____

We often call honest thoughts "giving someone the benefit of the doubt." Why is that important?

_____
_____
_____
_____
_____
_____
_____
_____

# 68. Leaders See the Good in ALL People

Great leaders see the good in people and acknowledge that everyone has something positive about them.

**WHY IS THIS IMPORTANT?**

We don't always get along with everyone. We don't always agree with or like people. But being able to see the good in people keeps us positive and is the right thing to do.

**RECOMMENDATION:**

Identify something good in the people around you. In a group, tape pieces of paper on the backs of everyone in your group. Everyone walks around and writes something positive on each other's backs. Then you can remove the paper from your back and read all the positive comments people wrote about you.

# Reflect & Complete

Think about someone you don't like and try to think about something positive about them. Maybe they are athletic or smart.

♥ _____
_____
_____
_____

♥ _____
_____
_____
_____

♥ _____
_____
_____
_____

# 69. Leaders Know How to Enjoy Their Time Off

It is okay not to have the radio on in the car. It's okay not to have the technology on. Enjoying time includes connecting to the people around you when you are not studying or working.

### Why is this important?

As technology evolves and invades every aspect of our lives, it's easy to get lost and disconnected from our loved ones. Enjoying our time off from school and work intentionally lets us: (1) rest and rejuvenate, (2) reconnect in our relationships, and (3) generate new ideas.

### Recommendation:

Set a goal to turn off everything, including your technology, for at least an hour a day.

**Make a list of things you like to do or journal during your time off, and share it with your friends and family.**

**This is a great way to connect and generate meaningful conversations.**

*Early Life Leadership Workbook*

# The icons are examples.

**Please note your leadership ideas for each icon. Write your experience or whatever comes to mind.**

🛒 _____

_____

_____

_____

🗺️ _____

_____

_____

_____

🎵 _____

_____

_____

_____

🐕🐈 _____

_____

_____

_____

Early Life Leadership Workbook

👥 _____
_____
_____
_____

🎣 _____
_____
_____

# 70. Leaders Have Good Manners

Good manners are easy to learn and will take you far in life.

**WHY IS THIS IMPORTANT?**

Having good manners shows social awareness, respect, and even charisma. These traits are all necessary to be effective leaders.

**RECOMMENDATION:**

The most effective way to learn good manners is through modeling and role-playing.

### What do good manners look like?

### Only use verbs to describe what good manners look like.

_____
_____
_____
_____
_____
_____
_____
_____
_____

# 71. Leaders Understand the Importance of Honor

*H*onor means you value the unsaid law of what is right, and you are willing to fight for what is right.

**WHY IS THIS IMPORTANT?**

We are often in the mindset of doing what is right or beneficial for us, not worrying about what is right for all. As leaders, we do what is right for all. When you understand honor, you respect and do what is right for all participants honoring the goals and vision of the group.

**RECOMMENDATION:**

There are many books, movies, biographies, and videos that tell the stories of people who demonstrated honor. Because this is such an abstract concept, I recommend you use a visual.

**Write about a time you had to honor something. Making the decision to do the right thing sometimes is hard. Maybe you protected a fellow student from a bully by reporting it to an adult, or anonymously reported students who were cheating in a class.**

_____
_____
_____
_____

# 72. Leaders Understand There Are Always Consequences to Their Actions

Great leaders understand there will always be consequences to their actions, both good and bad.

**WHY IS THIS IMPORTANT?**

In life, we know for every action there is a reaction, but great leaders take this very seriously. They understand their decisions have effects on their followers and on their organizations. For example, when employers cut jobs, it doesn't just affect the employees; it also affects their families.

**RECOMMENDATION:**

Think about a time you made a decision and had to deal with the consequences of your actions. Was it good or bad? Would you do things differently?

# What is the difference between good and bad consequences? Is there such a thing?

# How do you use consequences to make decisions?

# 73. Leaders Understand the Difference between Management and Leadership

Many do not realize there is a big difference between management and leadership. In management, one monitors processes and procedures. In leadership, we inspire and motivate to get the very best of our team members.

### Why is this important?

Understanding the difference between management and leadership is essential. Research shows that inspiration and motivation are more effective in the workplace than management.

### Recommendation:

Take ten minutes to do online research on the differences between leadership and management.

**Share a time you managed and a time you led.**

**What was the difference for you?**

Management: _____
_____
_____
_____
_____
_____

Leadership: _____
_____
_____
_____
_____
_____
_____

# 74. Leaders Understand the Importance of Denying Gratification

Great leaders understand that we must deny ourselves things to accomplish something bigger and better.

**WHY IS THIS IMPORTANT?**

For example, only by denying ourselves goodies can we lose weight. Only by turning off the television can we get our homework done. Great leaders understand that giving up the easy things in life will help us go further in life.

**RECOMMENDATION:**

There are two impactful things you can ask yourself to deny yourself instant gratification: (1) "Is this making me better?" and (2) "Is this going to help me accomplish my goals?"

## What is something that comes to mind instantly that you feel you need to decrease or give up in order to accomplish your goals?

# Reflect & Complete

Sandra is a mom of three. Each one of her children is a leader in the home. John (14) is the head chef, Jonah (10) is the technology guru, and Jazlyn (6) is the organization specialist. She likes to organize the shoes, the pillows on the couch, and the kitchen cabinets. Who are the leaders in your life, and what are their responsibilities?

# Person:

_____

# Leadership Responsibility:

## Person:

_____

## Leadership Responsibility:

# Person:

_____

# Leadership Responsibility:

## Person:

_____

## Leadership Responsibility:

# Person:

## Leadership Responsibility:

## Person:

_____

## Leadership Responsibility:

## Person:

_____

## Leadership Responsibility:

# Person:

_____

# Leadership Responsibility:

# 75. Leaders Understand the Art of Persuasion

Leaders understand the influence of the art of persuasion. They respectfully persuade people in their opinions, attitudes, purposes, motivations, or actions.

**WHY IS THIS IMPORTANT?**

Many will agree that persuasion is an art. As adult leaders, we persuade all day. This is a skill that all great leaders have mastered.

**RECOMMENDATION:**

Persuasion can be done through role-playing, during dinnertime discussions, and through school fundraisers. Sometimes when we are selling something like candy bars or crafts, we must persuade buyers that they are contributing to a good cause.

## When have you ever had to persuade someone to do something?

## What was it, and how did it turn out?

_____
_____
_____
_____
_____

# 76. Leaders Seek Advice

Great leaders seek advice because they understand these truths: (1) "I don't know everything," (2) "Making decisions based on data is crucial," and (3) "My idea might not be the best."

**WHY IS THIS IMPORTANT?**

Seeking advice from others creates trust, respect, unity, and buy-in within organizations. When we're looking for advice from others, it strengthens our relationships. This will set the platform for great things!

**RECOMMENDATION:**

Think about a time when you asked for advice. In your group or with your partner, explain why asking for advice is important.

## Who are the people in your life you ask for advice, and what is special about that person that makes their opinion valuable?

_____
_____
_____
_____

_____
_____
_____

Early Life Leadership Workbook

_____
_____
_____
_____

_____
_____
_____
_____

# 77. Great Leaders Lead by Example

As a leader, you realize the importance of setting a good example for your team by being respectful, hardworking, and goal-focused.

**WHY IS THIS IMPORTANT?**

A leader must be able to walk the walk and talk the talk. For example, if you do not allow social media during meetings and tell people to stay off their cell phones, yet you use your own cell phone, followers will lose respect for you.

**RECOMMENDATION:**

During group or team time, set some rules you will follow as a leader to set an example. For example, as a leader: (1) I will listen and respect everyone's opinion, (2) I will do what is best for the group, and (3) I will stay off my phone and stay focused on our team goals.

### What are some examples you try to set within your home or team?

Early Life Leadership Workbook

🎯 _____

_____
_____
_____
_____

🏆 _____

_____
_____
_____
_____

♥ _____

_____
_____
_____
_____

# 78. Leaders Are Teachable

Nobody likes a know-it-all, and no one knows it all. Leaders are lifelong learners, always willing to learn something new.

**WHY IS THIS IMPORTANT?**

Being teachable makes you a wonderful leader, learner, and person. Things are always changing, and great leaders understand that to be the best they must keep learning.

**RECOMMENDATION:**

To be teachable, we must: (1) listen, (2) be open-minded to the ideas of others, (3) seek new information in areas where we need to improve. Learning is everywhere! Be open to taking an interest in something new, exploring new hobbies, and exploring different books and publications.

What does being teachable mean, and why is it important?

_____
_____
_____
_____
_____

How do you know someone is teachable? What does teachable look like?

_____
_____
_____
_____
_____

# 79. Leaders Embrace Opportunity

Opportunity is all around us. There are always opportunities to make friends, find a job, get a positive reference letter, be healthier, learn something new, and just be better.

**Why is this important?**

Leaders need to see opportunity in everything because it's the way we grow, learn, create ideas, take risks, and meet new people.

**Recommendation:**

The biggest and most effective recommendation is practice. When things don't go as planned, you can say things like, "Ok, things didn't go as planned, but this is a great opportunity for us to _____. What other opportunities do you see?"

## What are some opportunities you have embraced?

## What do you need to increase or decrease to embrace the opportunities around you?

# Reflect & Complete

Think about what you have learned so far.

Please complete the next few pages.

_____ + _____ = 

## Leadership

## How do I see leadership?

_____
_____
_____
_____
_____
_____
_____
_____
_____
_____
_____
_____
_____
_____
_____
_____
_____
_____
_____

_____ + _____ =

## Team Leadership

How do I lead when I am playing on a team?

_____
_____
_____
_____
_____
_____
_____
_____
_____
_____
_____
_____
_____
_____
_____
_____
_____
_____

_____ + _____ =

## Family Leadership

### How do I lead in my home?

_____ + _____ = 

# Group Leadership

## How do I lead when I am in a group?

*Early Life Leadership Workbook*

_____ + _____ =

# Classroom Leadership

## How do I lead in the classroom?

_____ + _____ =

## Community Leadership

How do I lead in the community? (church, volunteering)

_____ + _____ =

## Employment/Service Leadership

How do I lead when I am working or providing a service?
(cutting the yard, part-time job)

---
---
---
---
---
---
---
---
---
---
---
---
---
---
---
---
---

_____ + _____ =

## Peer Leadership

### How do I lead when I am with my friends?

# 80. Leaders Understand the Importance of Being Healthy

**G**ood health is the foundation for our productivity and idea generation.

**WHY IS THIS IMPORTANT?**

When you are a leader, you make your health a priority just as you do your job and goals. How can you lead efficiently and be dependable if you are sick?

**RECOMMENDATION:**

Set health goals like: (1) drinking eight cups of water a day, (2) running or walking a 5K, and (3) limiting junk food and fast food.

**What are some of your current health goals or best practices?**

**What do you need to increase or decrease to be healthier?**

# 81. Leaders Give Compliments

Giving compliments to your followers or the people on your team makes everyone feel good.

**WHY IS THIS IMPORTANT?**

When someone provides you with a sincere compliment, it makes you feel appreciated and respected. When we feel good, we tend to work harder for our families, teachers, and employers.

**RECOMMENDATION:**

Make it a goal to give at least one sincere compliment a day.

## What is one of the best compliments you have ever received?

## What do you need to increase or decrease to give more compliments?

# Reflect & Complete

# How can I make my community better?

1. WHAT CAREER GOALS DO I HAVE?
_____
_____
_____
_____

2. WHAT ARE THE NEEDS OF MY COMMUNITY?
_____
_____
_____
_____

3. WHAT AM I PASSIONATE ABOUT?
_____
_____
_____
_____

4. HOW MUCH TIME CAN I COMMIT?
_____
_____
_____
_____

# 82. Leaders Persevere

The best leaders learn to handle failure gracefully because they know falling means you get right back up.

**WHY IS THIS IMPORTANT?**

It's important to understand things won't always be perfect. Not all of our plans go as we planned, and we don't always meet our goals. We live, learn, and move forward. We move forward no matter how hard it looks or how difficult it may be.

**RECOMMENDATION:**

There are some great books and movies with meaningful lessons on this. They remind us to persevere when we want to give up. Sometimes, before we learn to persevere, we get frustrated and hurt, but it's only temporary. We need to move on and reflect on what went right and what went wrong and then get back up again.

## Share a time when you persevered.

## What do you need to increase or decrease to handle failure gracefully?

# 83. Leaders Know the Importance of Building Negotiation Skills

*E*very good leader knows the art of negotiation and compromise.

### Why is this important?

As leaders, we negotiate sales prices, purchase prices, and employment contracts. Sometimes, we must compromise and meet each other halfway. As leaders, we always want everyone to feel like he or she won.

### Recommendation:

Instead of giving a firm yes or no to a request, make an offer and allow the other person to provide a counteroffer. Try role-playing.

**What is something you negotiate on a regular basis?**

**When have you negotiated something, and what was the compromise?**

_____
_____
_____
_____

# Reflect & Complete

What are four of your leadership accomplishments?

Frame them in the leadership gallery!

# 84. Leaders Reward Their Team Members

Everyone loves to be rewarded. When we reward our followers, we are acknowledging their hard work and dedication.

**WHY IS THIS IMPORTANT?**

Rewards come in different forms such as praise, thank-you notes, and group recognition. As leaders, we understand that by rewarding followers, we create respect, affirmation, and trust.

**RECOMMENDATION:**

Reward the people around you for their love and support. Reward your grandma for making Sunday breakfast or reward your mom for taking and picking you up from practice. We all like to be rewarded. A reward can look like a card or letter, a hug, and thank-you, or do something nice for someone in return for what he or she has done for you.

## How have you rewarded the people in your life?

## How does it make you feel?

_____
_____
_____
_____
_____

# 85. Leaders Do Not Participate in Favoritism

We don't always look to favor specific people, but sometimes leaders fall into the trap of picking the same people for special projects. By favoring people, we are overlooking the qualities and talents of others because they get along better with those they favor. This can be poisonous in the workplace.

**WHY IS THIS IMPORTANT?**

It is important to understand that we all have value. We all have something to contribute. It's okay to like certain people or have best friends, but we need to be open to knowing everyone in our group or team.

**RECOMMENDATION:**

Some things you can do to avoid favoritism include: (1) getting to know others in your group or team, (2) being mindful of other people's feelings, and (3) making sure you are fair and include everyone.

## What are some other problems one can have if they show favoritism?

## What do you need to increase or decrease to make everyone feel equal?

# 86. Leaders Can Say No Respectfully

As leaders, we cannot say yes to everything. We need to stay focused and prioritize the activities and commitments that we choose in our lives.

**WHY IS THIS IMPORTANT?**

In the real world, there is a lot going on. People ask us to volunteer, coach teams, donate money, join the softball team, and so on. It's important we only take on what we can handle and respectfully say no to things we can't.

**RECOMMENDATION:**

Think about your life and all the things you need to say no to in order to be successful in school—for example: (1) staying up late on the phone, (2) using drugs and alcohol, (3) bullying or putting people down, and (4) copying homework or cheating on a test. Try role-playing some of these things we need to say no to.

## When have you had to say no respectfully, and how did you feel? What do you need to increase or decrease to be more respectful?

# 87. Leaders Roll Up Their Sleeves and Get to Work

Great leaders aren't afraid to work hard and get things done.

**WHY IS THIS IMPORTANT?**

Rolling up your sleeves and getting to work is important because it establishes respect, promotes learning, and keeps you humble. Great leaders should be able to execute/perform most of the jobs within the organization.

**RECOMMENDATION:**

Get out of your comfort zone! Set aside gender and age. Help and put in some hard work by helping with the laundry, yard work, cooking, picking up, and cleaning the car.

## What are some of your experiences with hard work?

## What do you need to increase or decrease to get more work done?

## Reflect & Complete

Let's write an acrostic poem! Each line of the poem should consist of a word or phrase related to you and your leadership abilities.

**L**

**E**

**A**

**D**

**E**

**R**

# 88. Leaders Are Diligent

*D*iligence is caring about your performance and being conscientious in one's duties.

**WHY IS THIS IMPORTANT?**

Being diligent is important because we need to take pride in everything we do. We need to be diligent with our jobs and education. Great leaders try to give their best.

**RECOMMENDATION:**

Talk to the people in your life about being diligent. What were their experiences, and how did being diligent make them better?

## What are three things you are diligent about?

## What do you need to decrease and increase to be more diligent?

# 89. Leaders Practice Confident Communication

When you go to a restaurant, do you place your order with the waiter or does someone do it for you? Leaders can communicate confidently.

**WHY IS THIS IMPORTANT?**

You can turn a simple dinner into a confidence-building exercise by speaking directly to the servers. This will encourage you to speak directly to servers and increase your self-confidence when it comes to communicating effectively and respectfully.

**RECOMMENDATION:**

As you grow up, it is important that you learn to be more vocal. If you have questions at school, talk to your teachers, counselors, or principals. Try to handle things on your own instead of having your parents come to school. When you start college, your professors are not always going to be able to help you. Let your family know what your questions are but try to handle them on your own first.

## What is something you handled on your own in confidence?

## Were you successful? Why or why not?

_____
_____
_____
_____

# 90. Leaders Understand Loyalty

When you are loyal, you are committed to a person or goal.

**WHY IS THIS IMPORTANT?**

Loyalty to our team creates trust, respect, and unity. Not only is it important to be loyal to people, but we also need to be loyal to our goals and dreams. Loyalty is the key to maintaining lifelong friendships and accomplishing our goals.

**RECOMMENDATION:**

Be loyal to those who are loyal to you. Think about the people who are loyal to you. What does their loyalty look like? Will they help you when you need it? Are they there for you when you are feeling down? Are you loyal to them? Maybe you are loyal to your family, church, team, coach, or childhood friends.

## With a partner or group, talk about someone you are loyal to and why.

## What did that person do to earn your loyalty?

_____
_____
_____
_____
_____

# 9-1. Leaders Love Life

The great leaders from history and today will no doubt tell you they love what they do for a living and they love their lives. To be an effective leader, you need to learn to embrace life and love it!

**WHY IS THIS IMPORTANT?**

When you love your life, that happiness carries over to other parts of your life.

**RECOMMENDATION:**

Some people create posters with all the things they love in their lives as a reminder when things get hard. Others journal or keep a gratitude list.

## What are ten things you love about your life?

1. _____
2. _____
3. _____
4. _____
5. _____
6. _____
7. _____
8. _____
9. _____
10. _____

# 9.2. Leaders Follow the Rules

*G*reat leaders follow the rules because they know they set the example for everyone else.

**WHY IS THIS IMPORTANT?**

How effective can you be if other people see you not following the rules you want them to follow?

**RECOMMENDATION:**

Be the leader you would want to lead you. Follow the rules. Remember rules are there based on past problems and safety. It is the right thing to do even when you don't agree.

## What are some things you need to increase or decrease to make it easier to follow the rules?

# 9.3. Leaders Give the Whole Team Credit

As leaders, we never achieve anything alone. Give credit where it is due.

**WHY IS THIS IMPORTANT?**

Giving credit to your team increases job satisfaction and builds team unity and trust.

**RECOMMENDATION:**

When you are part of a study group or a team: (1) make sure you say "we" instead of "I;" (2) if you are complimented, remind them you are part of a team; and (3) give your team praise and positive energy.

## What are some things that can go wrong if you take all the credit?

_____
_____
_____
_____
_____
_____
_____

# 9.4. Leaders Understand the Power of Words

Words can make someone feel good, or they can quickly bring someone down. Leaders choose their words wisely.

**WHY IS THIS IMPORTANT?**

As leaders, we are often talking all day. Are you paying attention to what you are saying? Are you saying positive things to your family, friends, and teachers? Remember, negative comments hurt relationships, lack integrity, and make you look bad. It is important that we think about what we say before we say it.

**RECOMMENDATION:**

Find a family member or friend and practice different scenarios. "You're dumb" versus "I don't agree; does anyone have any other ideas?"; "I hate that idea," versus, "I think all ideas have potential, so how can we make this one better?"

## Has anyone ever told you anything that hurt you?

## Why did it hurt, and how can we prevent that from happening to someone else?

_____

_____

_____

# 95. Leaders Wear All Kinds of Different Hats

In life, we all wear different hats. We are leaders, secretaries, students, custodians, coaches, mechanics, gardeners, and caregivers. We do different things in all the different parts of our lives.

**WHY IS THIS IMPORTANT?**

In life, we must be able to adjust to different situations and people.

**RECOMMENDATION:**

There are three ways to understand the importance of wearing different hats: (1) think about the different hats that affect your everyday life, (2) take an opportunity to wear the different hats by participating in different activities, and (3) be intentional with your time and words. For example, Sam defines the tasks in her home to the kids: "We all are janitors and clean. We are all cooks and help prepare dinner. We are all gardeners and help pull weeds and rake leaves."

**What are the most and least favorite hats you wear?**

_____
_____
_____
_____
_____

# 96. Leaders Are Compassionate

*B*eing compassionate helps leaders build healthy relationships with followers. It reinforces empathy and shows leaders as more human.

**WHY IS THIS IMPORTANT?**

When we are compassionate, we can feel what others are feeling. This doesn't mean we are weak. It means we are human and we are trying to put ourselves in other people's shoes. Over the years, I have lost students to car accidents, drug overdoses, suicide, and illness. I have also had the privilege to work with great professionals who have suffered from cancer and other hardships. As a team, we all pulled together to raise money, buy flowers, and get the work done for the absent coworker.

**RECOMMENDATION:**

Find a passion for compassion! Noah is a runner. He and his son collect old shoes and donate them to their local church who take them to orphanages in Mexico. They show their compassion by getting involved and helping tend to the needs of others. Noah wants him to see that there are people less fortunate than him.

## What three things do you have compassion for?

1. _____
2. _____
3. _____

*Early Life Leadership Workbook*

# Future Leadership Goals Checklist

- [ ] Read More
- [ ] Set Goals and Make a Plan on How to Accomplish Them
- [ ] Improve My Family Relationships
- [ ] Overcome My Shyness
- [ ] Learn to Accept Criticism
- [ ] Volunteer in My Community
- [ ] Be a Better Listener
- [ ] Be a Better Public Speaker
- [ ] Show Others I Appreciate Them
- [ ] _____
- [ ] _____
- [ ] _____
- [ ] _____
- [ ] _____
- [ ] _____
- [ ] _____
- [ ] _____
- [ ] _____

# 97. Leaders Understand the Importance of a Good Tribe

A tribe is the group of people around you who are trustworthy, care for you, and make you better.

**WHY IS THIS IMPORTANT?**

Life is hard and full of questions. It is important that we surround ourselves with people who can be there for us when we need help, advice, a listening ear, or comfort and support during hard times.

**RECOMMENDATION:**

Your tribe doesn't have to be a bunch of friends from the same group. Adults also call this an inner circle. Your tribe, or inner circle, can be family members, teachers, coaches, pastors, and friends. Your tribe should be made up of different people of all ages and backgrounds. This will give you a variety of advice and perspectives.

## Who are the people in your tribe, and how do they make you better?

## What do you need to increase or decrease to strengthen your tribe?

# 9-8. Leaders Know They Cannot Control Others, Only Themselves

Leaders understand some people they are trying to lead will want to go in another direction.

**WHY IS THIS IMPORTANT?**

As leaders, we expect to "make things happen" or "be catalysts for change," but even the greatest leaders will tell you that no matter how great or inspirational you are, there will be at least one who won't budge. Remember we can't control other people.

**RECOMMENDATION:**

It is essential to understand not everyone is going to want to be your friend, and that's okay. Just move on and find another friend.

**It is normal to be upset sometimes, but what can you increase or decrease in your life when you cannot control the actions of others?**

# 9-9. Leaders Love What They Do

Leaders love what they do and do what they love.

**WHY IS THIS IMPORTANT?**

Dissatisfaction is toxic. When someone is unhappy, it sinks through to other areas of his or her life. When we are not happy, it is extremely noticeable to others. Loving what you do in important because your passion will launch you toward success.

**RECOMMENDATION:**

There are three things you need to understand:
(1) when you do something, do it with a glad heart.
(2) make a list of things you love to do.
(3) find family and friends who have the same interests.

## What are three things you love to do?

1. _____
_____
_____
_____
_____
_____

2. _____
_____
_____
_____
_____
_____
_____

3. _____
_____
_____
_____
_____
_____
_____

# 100. Leaders Respect Differences

Leaders respect different ideas, gender, race, disability, cultures, and religion.

**WHY IS THIS IMPORTANT?**

Leaders set the example. It is crucial that leaders respect differences. This encourages others to do the same thing. We do not have to agree with everything, but we need to respect differences.

**RECOMMENDATION:**

Instead of simply disagreeing with someone, get to know people with different ideas, genders, races, disabilities, and religions. Look for their strengths and good qualities.

## What do you need to increase or decrease in order to embrace differences in the world?

## What did you learn?

# 101. Leaders Reflect

Leaders understand that through the reflection process, they can learn, grow, and understand more.

**WHY IS THIS IMPORTANT?**

There is a lot of information coming at us. Through the reflection process, we can filter important information. Keep what makes us better, and filter what doesn't.

### What are 5 important things you learned from your leadership journey in this book?

# Bonus!

## Free Copy of the DeMara Reflection Grid

# Early Life Leadership Workbook

| Memorization Icon | "OW" Leadership Reflection | <u>Internalization</u><br>What does that look like? Draw a picture or symbol. | What do I need to do to nurture this area? |
|---|---|---|---|
|  | **Know:**<br>What do I know about Leadership? |  |  |
|  | **Glow:**<br>How do I stand out? |  |  |
|  | **Show:**<br>What do I show others? How do others perceive me? |  |  |
|  | **Grow:**<br>How am I growing as a leader? What am I doing to better my leadership skills? |  |  |

Early Life Leadership Workbook

| | | | |
|---|---|---|---|
| | **SNOW:** What is cold in my leadership life and requires attention? | | |
| | **BOWL:** What is in my bowl? What leadership resources do I have available to me? | | |
| | **MOW:** What is mowing me down and stopping me from moving to the next level of leadership greatness? | | |
| | **FLOW:** What is flowing smoothly? What are the things going well in the leadership aspect of my life? | | |
| | **TOW:** What am I towing that may be slowing me down from reaching my full leadership potential? | | |

EarlyLifeLeadership.com | 169

| | | | |
|---|---|---|---|
| | **Bow:** What am I ready to launch forward? | | |
| | **Low:** What is an area of weakness I need to work on? | | |
| | **Sow:** What am I working on? Remember, you reap what you sow. | | |
| | **Row:** What am I rowing toward? Am I going in the right direction? | | |
| | **Owe:** Whom do I owe for mentoring me? What am I taking away from my mentors? | | |

# Bibliography

Ackerman, D., & Barnett, W. (2005). Prepared for Kindergarten: What Does "Readiness" Mean? Preschool Policy Brief for the National Institute for Early Education Research, 13-13.

Addison, L., Oliver, A. I., & Cooper, C. R. (1987). Developing leadership potential in gifted children and youth. Reston, VA: ERIC Clearinghouse on Handicapped and Gifted Children.

Andersen, L. (2011). The effects of formal leadership-lessons on the emergence of positive social-leadership skills of pre-kindergarten students.

Asendorpf, J. B., & Van Aken, M. A. G. (2002). Validity of big five personality judgments in childhood: A 9-year longitudinal study; 17: 1-17 (2003).

Ayman, R., & Korabik, K. (2010). Leadership: Why gender and culture matter. American Psychologist, 65(3), 157.

Berkowitz, M. (2009). Character education and gifted children. High Ability Studies, 20(2), 131-142.

Bisland, A. (January 01, 2004). Developing Leadership Skills in Young Gifted Students. The Gifted Child Today, 27, 24-31.

Bohlin, L. C. (2000). Determinants of young children's leadership and dominance strategies during play. (9993607, Indiana University). ProQuest Dissertations and Theses. 139-139 p. Retrieved fromhttp://search.proquest.com/docview/304624371?accountid=7058. (304624371).

Boseovski, J. J., Shallwani, S., & Lee, K. (2009). It's all good: Children's personality attributions after repeated success and failure in peer and computer interactions. British Journal of Developmental Psychology, 27(4), 783-797.

Brenner, S. C. (1991). Leadership characteristics in young children as perceived by caregivers in a child care setting. Philadelphia, Pa.

Burchinal, M., Howes, C., Pianta, R., Bryant, D., Early, D., Clifford, R., & Barbarin, O. (2008). Predicting child outcomes at the end of kindergarten from the quality of pre-kindergarten teacher-child interactions and instruction. Applied Developmental Science, 12(3), 140-153.

Campbell, R. (2007, January 1). Leadership: Getting It Done. Retrieved September 6, 2014, from http://web.missouri.edu/~campbellr/Leadership/chapter4.htm

Carver, C. L. (2012). Developing Leadership Content Knowledge during School Leader Preparation. International Journal of Educational Leadership Preparation, 7(3),

Caspi, A., Harrington, H., Milne, B., Amell, J. W., Theodore, R. F., & Moffitt, T. E. (2003). Children's behavioral styles at age 3 are linked to their adult personality traits at age 26. Journal of Personality, 71(4), 495 - 513.

Castillo, C. T. (2001). The effects of a dual-language education program on student achievement and development of leadership abilities. (Order No. 3022340, Our Lady of the Lake University). ProQuest Dissertations and Theses, 77-77 p. Retrieved from
http://search.proquest.com/docview/251479399?accountid=7058. (251479399).

Centers for Disease Control and Prevention. (2012, June 08). Retrieved from
http://www.cdc.gov/mmwr/preview/mmwrhtml/ss6104a1.htm

Charlesworth, R. (1987). Understanding child development. (2nd ed.). Albany, New York: Delmar Publishers Inc.

Chetty, R., Friedman, J. N., Hilger, N., Saenz, E., Schanzenbach, D. W., & Yagan, D. (2010, November 1). $320,000 Kindergarten Teachers. Kappan, 22-25.

Chickering, A. & Gamson Z. 1987, "Seven principles for good practice in undergraduate education," Reprinted by Honolulu Community College, National Learning Infrastructure Initiative, 2003, Mapping the Learning Space: Design Implications, Educause, viewed 23 March 2004

Clotfelter, Charles T. & Ladd, Helen F. & Vigdor, Jacob L., 2007. "Teacher credentials and student achievement: Longitudinal analysis with student fixed effects," Economics of Education Review, Elsevier, vol. 26(6), pages 673-682, December

Colker, L. J. Twelve Characteristics of Early Childhood Teachers. Beyond the Journal: Young Children on the Web, 1-6.

Cummins, J. (2000). Language, power, and pedagogy bilingual children in the crossfire. Clevedon, England: Multilingual Matters

Dhuey, E., & Lipscomb, S. (2006). What Makes a Leader? Relative Age and High School Leadership. Economics of Education Review, 27(2), 173-183.

Do Kindergarten Teachers Make a Difference?. (2010, August 2). Retrieved February 21, 2014, from http://blog.columbiasocialenterprise.org/?p=1113

Eagly Johannesen-Schmidh and van Engen (2003) Transformational, transactional, and laissez-faire leadership styles: A meta-analysis comparing women and men. Psychological Bulletin, 129(4), 569-591.

Educational Testing Service (2012). Relationships between Big Five and Academic and Workforce Outcomes. Retrieved February 17, 2016, from

https://www.ets.org/s/workforce_readiness/pdf/21334_big_5.pdf

Ehrler, D. J., Evans, J. G. and McGhee, R. L. (1999), Extending Big-Five theory into childhood: A preliminary investigation into the relationship between Big-Five personality traits and behavior problems in children. Psychol. Schs., 36: 451–458. doi: 10.1002/(SICI)1520-6807(199911)36:6<451::AID-PITS1>3.0.CO;2-E

Fox, Deborah Lee, "Teachers' Perceptions of Leadership in Young Children" (2012). University of New Orleans Theses and Dissertations. Paper 1546. http://scholarworks.uno.edu/td/1546

French, D. C., & Stright, A. L. (1991). Emergent leadership in children's small groups. Small Group Research, 22(2), 187-199.

French, D. C., Waas, G. A., Stright, A. L., & Baker, J. A. (1986). Leadership asymmetries in mixed-age children's groups. Child Development, 1277-1283.

Fu, V. R. (1979). Preschool leadership-followership behaviors. Child Study Journal, 9(2), 133-140.

Fu, V. R. (1970). The development of a nursery school leadership observation schedule and a nursery school leadership rating scale.

Fukada, H., Fukada, S., & Hicks, J. (1997). The relationship between leadership and sociometric status among preschool children. The Journal of Genetic Psychology, 158(4), 481-486.

Genesee, F., & Paradis, J. (2004). Dual language development and disorders: A handbook on bilingualism and second language learning. Baltimore, Maryland: Paul H. Brookes Publishing.

Goldberg, L. R. (1993). The structure of phenotypic personality traits. American psychologist, 48(1), 26.

Gravetter, F., & Wallnau, L. (2009). Statistics for the behavioral sciences (8th ed.). Belmont, CA: Wadsworth.

Gullo, D. F., Heroman, C., & Copple, C., (2002). Teaching and Learning in the Kindergarten Year. K Today.

Guthrie, K., Jones, T., Hu, S., & Osteen, L. (2013). Cultivating leader identity and capacity in students from diverse backgrounds. Hoboken, NJ: Wiley Periodicals.

Hahn, E., Gottschling, J., & Spinath, F. M. (June 01, 2012). Short measurements of personality - Validity, and reliability of the GSOEP Big Five Inventory (BFI-S). Journal of Research in Personality, 46, 3, 355-359.

Hampson SE, Goldberg LR.; J Pers Soc Psychol. 2006 Oct;91(4):763-79.

Hampson SE, Goldberg LR, Vogt TM, Dubanoski JP., Health

Psychol. 2006 Jan;25(1):57-64. PMID: 16448298

Henry, M. (1998). The Manager's Job: Folklore and Fact. In Harvard Business Review on Leadership. Boston, Mass.: Harvard Business School Publishing.

Hensel, N. H. (1991). Social leadership skills in young children. Roeper Review, 14(1), 4.

Hess, L. (2010). Student leadership education in elementary classroom. San Rafael, Calif: Dominican University of California.

Honigsfeld, A., & Cohan, A. (2012). Breaking the Mold of Education for Culturally and Linguistically Diverse Students. Lanham, ML: Roman & Littlefield Education.

Howard, P., & Howard, J. (2001). The owner's manual for personality at work: How the big five personality traits affect performance, communication, teamwork, leadership, and sales. Marietta, GA: Bard Press.

Irby, B. J., & Lara-Alecio, R. (1996). Attributes of Hispanic Gifted Bilingual Students as Perceived by Bilingual Educators in Texas. SABE Journal, 11, 120-143.

Kirnon, S. N., & Pepperdine University. (2008). Inspiring citizenship and leadership: Youth citizenship seminar.

John, O. P., Naumann, L. P., & Soto, C. J. (2008). Paradigm Shift to the Integrative Big-Five Trait Taxonomy: History, Measurement, and Conceptual Issues. In O. P. John, R. W. Robins, & L. A. Pervin (Eds.), Handbook of personality: Theory and research (pp. 114-158). New York, NY: Guilford Press.

Judge, Timothy A.; Bono, Joyce E.; Ilies, Remus; Gerhardt, Megan W. Journal of Applied Psychology, Vol 87(4), Aug 2002, 765-780. doi: 10.1037/0021-9010.87.4.765

Judkins Jr., P. A. Certain criteria lead toward leadership. Operations and Planning Rural Health Association, Farming, Maine.

Karschney, K. J. (2003). Structured intergenerational dialogue: A multiple case study of eleven children in a leadership workshop. (Order No. 3106567, Gonzaga University).

ProQuest Dissertations and Theses, 261-261 p. Retrieved from http://search.proquest.com/docview/305278835?accountid=7058. (305278835).

Lamon, C. C., & Valdosta State University. (2005). The impact of the Georgia Pre-K Program on the achievement gap between at-risk and not-at-risk students for kindergarten readiness as measured by teacher perception and student assessments.

Lee, Y., & Recchia, S. L. (2008). "Who's the Boss?" Young Children's Power and Influence in an Early Childhood Classroom. Early Childhood Research & Practice, 10(1).

Lee, P., Lan, W., Wang, C., & Chiu, H. (2008). Helping Young Children to Delay Gratification. Early Childhood Education Journal, 35(6), 557-564.

Lester, J. E. (2002) Does Your Child Have Leadership Ability?. Ohio Leadership Institute.

Li, Y., Anderson, R. C., Nguyen-Jahiel, K., Dong, T., Archodidou, A., Kim, I. H., & Miller, B. (2007). Emergent leadership in children's discussion groups. Cognition and Instruction, 25(1), 1-2.

Lieberman, L. J., Arndt, K., & Daggett, S. (2007). Promoting leadership in physical education and recreation. Journal of Physical Education, Recreation & Dance, 78(3), 46-50.

MacLure, M., Jones, L., Holmes, R., & MacRae, C. (2012). Becoming a Problem: Behavior and Reputation in the Early Years Classroom. British Educational Research Journal, 38(3), 447-471.

Manley, M., & Northeastern University (Boston, Mass.). (2013). A mixed methods study on leadership, communication, cooperation, and collaboration in children enrolled in the learning leadership academy.

Markey, P. M., Markey, C. N., & Tinsley, B. J. (2004). Children's behavioral manifestations of the five-factor model of personality. Personality and Social Psychology Bulletin, 30(4), 423-432.

Mawson, B. (2011). Children's Leadership Strategies in Early Childhood. Journal of Research in Childhood Education, 25(4), 327-338.

Maynard, T., & Nigel, T. (2004). An introduction to early childhood studies. Thousand Oaks, California: Sage Publications Ltd.

Meriweather, S., & Karnes, F. A. (1989). Parents' Views on Leadership. Gifted Child Today (GCT), 12(1), 55-59.

Minnesota Early Childhood Teacher Educators. (1986). Kindergarten excellence: Knowledge and competencies of kindergarten teachers. St. Paul, MN: Minnesota Dept. of Education.

Murray, J., Theakston, A., & Wells, A. (2016). Can the attention training technique turn one marshmallow into two? Improving children's ability to delay gratification. Behavior Research and Therapy, 77, 34-39. doi:10.1016/j.brat.2015.11.009

National Society for the Gifted and Talented (2012). Giftedness defined - what is gifted & talented?. Retrieved from http://www.nsgt.org/articles/index.asp

Nelson, A. E. (January 01, 2010). In focus youth leadership— Stepping in early to grow great leaders. Leadership in Action, 29, 6, 20-24.

New Jersey Department of Education. (1999) Have Your Heard? The Truth About Kindergarten. A Guide to Understanding Kindergarten. url:http://www.nj.gov/education/ece/k/truth.pdf

Olivero, J. L.; Leading leaders. Nueva Learning Center.

Piaget, J. (1952). The origins of intelligence in children (Vol. 8, No. 5, p. 18). New York: International Universities Press.

Pandya, A. A., & Jogsan, Y. A. (2013). Personality and Locus of Control among School Children. Educational Research and Reviews, 8(22), 2193-2196.

Parmer, L. (2012). The relationship between personality and leadership in adolescents. (Order No. 3535621, Our Lady of the Lake University). ProQuest Dissertations and Theses, 201. Retrieved from http://search.proquest.com/docview/1283388608?accountid=7058. (1283388608).

Parten, M. B. (1933). Leadership among preschool children. The Journal of Abnormal and Social Psychology, 27(4), 430.

Prepared for Kindergarten: What Does "Readiness" Mean? Preschool Policy Brief for the National Institute for Early Education Research, 13-13.

Pramling Samuelsson, I., & Kaga, Y. (2008). The contribution of early childhood education to a sustainable society. Paris, UNESCO.

Lord, Robert G.; de Vader, Christy L.; Alliger, George M. Journal of Applied Psychology, Vol 71(3), Aug 1986, 402-410. http://dx.doi.org/10.1037/0021-9010.71.3.402

Leadership giftedness in preschool children. Roeper Review, 4, 3, 26-28.

Rios, L. A. (2010). The relationship between emerging leadership behavior in children and their academic performance. Our Lady of the Lake University). ProQuest Dissertations and Theses, http://search.proquest.com/docview/866567855?accountid=7058

Rogelberg, S. G. (Ed.). (2006). Encyclopedia of industrial and organizational psychology. Sage Publications.

Rushton, J. (1966). The relationship between personality characteristics and scholastics success in eleven-year-old children. The British Journal of Educational Psychology, 36(The University of Manchester), 178-183.

Russell, B., Londhe, R., & Britner, P. (2013). Parental Contributions to the Delay of Gratification in Preschool-aged Children. Journal of Child & Family Studies, 22(4), 471-478. doi:10.1007/s10826-012-9599-8

Ryan, K., & Cooper, J. (2010). Kaleidoscope: Contemporary and classic readings in education (12th ed.). Belmont, Calif.: Wadsworth Cengage Learning.

Scharf, M., & Mayseless, O. (2009). Socioemotional Characteristics of Elementary School Children Identified as Exhibiting Social Leadership Qualities. Journal of Genetic Psychology, 170(1), 73-94.

Schoenfeldt, K. R. (2012). Kindergarten program type as a predictor for reading achievement in third grade. (Doctoral dissertation), Available from ProQuest Dissertations & Theses.

Serafin, A. G. (1992). Charismatic Behaviors and Traits of Future Educational Leaders.

Shaunessy, E., & Karnes, F. A. (2004). Instruments for Measuring Leadership in Children and Youth. Gifted Child Today, 27(1), 42-47.

Shipley, G. L. (1998). Early childhood educators' perceptions of kindergarten readiness in a southern Ohio school district: Implications for educational leadership.

Short, D., & Echevarria, J. (2005). Teacher Skill to Support English Language Learners. The Best of Educational Leadership 2004-2005, 62, 8-13.

Silverman, L. K. (2000). Counseling the gifted and talented. (1 ed.). Denver, CO: Love Publishing Company.

Soffler, A. A. (2011). What is the Nature of Children's Leadership in Early Childhood Educational Settings? A Grounded Theory. Fort Collins, Co.: Colorado State University.

Srivastava, S. (2015). Measuring the Big Five Personality Factors. Retrieved March 18, 2015 from http://psdlab.uoregon.edu/bigfive.html.

Stark, P. (Ed.). (2014, July 1). Glossary of Statistical Terms. Retrieved from http://www.stat.berkeley.edu/~stark/SticiGui/Text/gloss.htm#categorical

Texas English Language Learners Portal. (2012). Retrieved December 27, 2015.

The development of markers for the Big-Five factor structure. Goldberg, Lewis R. Psychological Assessment, Vol 4(1), Mar 1992, 26-42. doi: 10.1037/1040-3590.4.1.26

Trawick-Smith, J. (1988). "Let's say you're the baby, OK?" Play leadership and following behavior of young children. Young Children.

Villagomez, E. T. (2007). An inductive analysis of the self-perceptions of young children related to leadership as a construct. Our Lady of the Lake University). ProQuest Dissertations and Theses,http://search.proquest.com/docview/304717742?accountid=7058

Vygotsky, L. S. (1967). Play and its role in the mental development of the child. Journal of Russian and East European Psychology, 5(3), 6-18.

Wells, C. (1986). The meaning makers: Children learning language and using language to learn (1st ed.). Portsmouth, N.H.: Heinemann.

2013 Social Enterprise Conference, Columbia Business School. (2013, January 1). Do Kindergarten Teachers Make a Difference?. Retrieved, from http://blog.columbiasocialenterprise.org/

# About the Author

Christina DeMara is the idealistic creator and author of the two leadership doctrines coined as *Meaningful Leadership* and *Early Life Leadership*. Above that, she is a Christian, mother, wife, and, educator, public speaker, curriculum creative, and promoter of giving. Her first job, as a high school dropout, was at fifteen, working for the Kirby Vacuum Company. She later completed her bachelor's degree in Interdisciplinary Studies with a minor in Special Education where she found a deep passion for teaching students with exceptionalities. She proudly holds three master's degrees in Special Education, Educational Administration and Leadership, and a third in Curriculum and Instruction from the University of Texas-Rio Grande Valley. She later studied business and leadership extensively through Our Lady of the Lake University in San Antonio, Texas. She has experienced and studied leadership theory, organizational models, and business strategy. She is best known for her creative ideal formulation, and interactive books, *Early Life Leadership Workbook for Girls*, and *I'm Not Broken: The Power of Prayer, Scripture, and Interactive Journaling*. Christina DeMara has overcome many obstacles in life through the grace of God and tries every day to motivate others. She enjoys spending time with her family, going to the beach, church, cooking, research, teaching, do-it-yourself projects, and trying new restaurants.

# Please Connect with Christina!

## She would love to hear from you!

Christina has two Facebook groups called

***I Love Reading & Writing***

and

***I Love Leadership***

for her readers.

You are welcome to join!

# Bless This Book!

If you enjoyed this book or any other of Christina's books, your honest review is greatly appreciated! Reviews help the author's books be seen by others and help the writer qualify for different book promotions.

## Your Time and Review is Appreciated

### Questions?

ChristinaDeMara.com
EarlyLifeLeadership.com
christinademara@gmail.com

# Also by Christina DeMara

*My Prayer Book*

**Peace is Mine**
The Forgiveness Journal

**I'm Not Broken**
The Power of Prayer, Scripture, and Interactive Journaling

**How God Saved Me**
My Mother's Memoirs on Abuse, Depression & Overeating

**The I Am Journal**
A Soul-Searching Journal for Creative Women of God

**Isaiah 43:2**
40 Days of Scriptures, Reflection, and Journaling for the Lent Season

# Christina DeMara's Meaningful Journal & Resources

### Meaningful Leadership
How to Build Indestructible Relationships with Your Team Members Through Intentionality and Faith

### Meaningful Leadership Journal

### Meaningful Leadership Prayer Journal

### Meaningful Teacher Leadership
Reflection, Refinement, and Student Achievement

### Meaningful Writing & Self-Publishing
Your Guide to Igniting Your Pen, Faith, Creativity & Entrepreneurship

Made in the USA
Coppell, TX
23 October 2020